"You're about **"You thi**

"Let's just say that some highly experienced caregivers have resigned," Ty said.

"I'll make it work." She wrapped both hands around the coffee mug and stared into its depths. *I have to!*

Her son providentially entered the kitchen at that moment. "Mr. Matthews's grandmother said that I could have hot chocolate. Is that right?"

"Sure." Ty got up. "I'll show you where things are and you can make it yourself from now on."

"Cool." Danny followed Ty from the refrigerator to the silverware drawer to the cupboard like a shadow.

He hadn't been around many men. Hannah hadn't really dated anyone since her husband died. Watching her little boy glue himself to Ty Matthews, she realized how much Danny must have missed father-son contact.

"Cute kid," Ty whispered. "He'll probably do a lot to improve my grandmother's mood. She really is partial to little boys. I was just as adorable as a kid."

She observed his blue eyes twinkle. In her book, he was still pretty adorable.

Books by Judy Baer

Love Inspired

Be My Neat-Heart
Mirror, Mirror
Sleeping Beauty
The Cinderella List
Mending Her Heart
The Bachelor Boss

Steeple Hill Single Title

The Whitney Chronicles
Million Dollar Dilemma
Norah's Ark

JUDY BAER

Angel Award–winning author and two-time RITA®
Award finalist Judy Baer has written more than seventy books in the past twenty years. A native of North
Dakota and graduate of Concordia College in Minnesota, she currently lives near Minneapolis. In addition to writing, Judy works as a personal life coach
and writing coach. Judy speaks in churches, libraries,
women's groups and at writers' conferences across
the country. She enjoys time with her husband, two
daughters, three stepchildren and the growing number of spouses, pets and babies they bring home. Judy,
who once raised buffalo, now owns horses. She recently completed her master's degree and accepted a
position as adjunct faculty at St. Mary's University,
Minneapolis, Minnesota. Readers are invited to visit
her website at www.judykbaer.com.

The Bachelor Boss

Judy Baer

Love Inspired

Recycling programs for this product may not exist in your area.

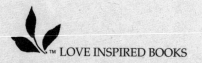

™ LOVE INSPIRED BOOKS

ISBN-13: 978-0-373-81640-8

THE BACHELOR BOSS

www.LoveInspiredBooks.com

Printed in U.S.A.

Honor your father and your mother,
so that your days may be long in the land
that the Lord is giving you.
—*Exodus* 20:12

This was written in honor of my parents and all the wise and wonderful older people I've had in my life.

Chapter One

White-knuckled with anxiety, Hannah St. James pulled her car into the parking lot of the Marshall medical complex. She wasn't the kind to beg, but she would if she had to. She'd never needed a job as badly as she did now, and she'd do whatever it took to get one.

Her mind still on losing her job at Family Affairs, a caregiving service for the elderly, she didn't even see the Mercedes until their fenders met.

Hazel eyes wide, she slipped out of her old Kia just as an attractive, dark-haired man emerged from the obscenely shiny Mercedes and strode toward her. His broad shoulders were rigid and his handsome jaw set. Anger fairly oozed off of him.

"You drove right into me," he said in astonishment. His eyes were hidden behind sunglasses and no doubt shooting darts.

He was an undeniably good-looking man. His finely chiseled features reminded her of her late husband, Steve. She guessed he was about her own age—in his early thirties. She fleetingly wished that she'd met him under different, more friendly, circumstances.

She forced that thought to the back of her mind. "I was distracted. I'm sorry." She stared at the fenders of the two cars. The Mercedes had a ding, without a doubt, but the front of her little car looked as if it had been through a trash masher. "I have insurance."

She didn't add that it was liability insurance, which would pay for the Mercedes but not for her old clunker. Now, at least, the hail damage it had suffered would not be so noticeable. All eyes would be fixed on her fender.

"This car is six weeks old," the man muttered. "Six weeks!" He took off his glasses to reveal blue eyes with long, dark lashes.

"Mine is eight years," Hannah said absently as she pulled at one of her red curls. He probably had other cars he could use while his was in the shop. She'd be taking the bus, if she had anywhere to go now that she was unemployed. *Unemployed.* She groaned inwardly. It would certainly be a mess getting to job interviews without a car.

"Ty, dear, is everything okay?" The car's passenger-side window opened and a white-haired woman with piercing blue eyes peered out.

"It's okay, Gram. We'll take care of it."

Hannah stared in horror at the old woman. She looked fragile. What if she'd been hurt? Hannah raced to the woman's window before she could close it.

"I am so sorry. Are you okay? How does your neck feel?" All Hannah's geriatric nursing skills flooded to the surface. "Do you need to go to the hospital?"

"Mercy no, dear. I'm fine. Besides, I'm here to see my doctor." The wizened woman gestured toward the medical building. "He can look at me. I'm sure he'll say all is well. Thank you for being so concerned."

"Well, she did hit our car," the man pointed out tersely, less forgiving than the old woman. His blue eyes were just like his grandmother's, Hannah noted. Only he had unbelievably long, dark lashes. Very nice. Actually, more than nice. She surprised herself. It had been a long time since she'd noticed much of anything about the opposite sex.

"But see how remorseful she is."

"Insurance companies don't care about remorse, Grams."

Hannah dug a piece of paper and pen from her pocket and began to scribble. "Here is my email address and the name of my insurance company."

He took it without reading it and stuffed it in his pocket. With a sigh, he pulled a business card from the inside pocket of his jacket and handed it to Hannah. *TDM Imports and Exports*.

"My insurance agent will be in touch," she ventured.

"He'd better be."

Hannah winced. She watched him get into the car, pull forward and park in the handicapped space nearest the door. He then lovingly extracted the tiny white-haired woman from the front seat and lifted her in his arms as a nurse from the clinic appeared with a wheelchair. Gently, he placed the old woman in the chair and they moved away.

"Be still my heart," Hannah murmured as unexpected emotions rushed through her. It wasn't because he was good-looking, though he was, or that he was tall and athletically built, a fact revealed when he shrugged out of his winter coat as he followed his grandmother's wheelchair into the building. It wasn't because his dark brown hair was the kind of hair a woman could happily run her fingers through. What made Hannah's heart go pitty-pat was the sight of a man so concerned and gentle with an elderly woman. For a geriatric nurse like Hannah, it was a joy to see.

Then the enormity of her own problems returned and her thoughts focused on more pressing issues. She'd lost her job through no fault of her own. She was behind on her bills and had no money left in savings. After this accident, her car insurance would probably go up. She'd have to find a way to repair her battered car. And her younger sister Trisha's tuition for summer school would be due before she knew it. The girl had been going to school year round in order to finish quickly. After today, there was no way Trisha could finish soon enough for Hannah.

She got back into her car, crossed her arms over the steering wheel, rested her head on her forearms and allowed the hot tears she'd been holding back to fall. Hannah allowed herself only a few moments of self-pity, however, before she wiped away her running mascara and got back out of her car. She'd have to worry about this later. Right now, she had bigger fish to fry.

When God closes a door He opens a window. *A window will open, a window will open*... she told herself as she raced up the stairs to Dr. Phillip Harvey's office.

An internist physician who specialized in geriatrics, Doc Harvey had been a close friend of her parents and, later, of hers. The office, with its commercial-grade brown carpeting, beige walls and wildlife prints, was familiar. Little had changed since she'd worked here as a receptionist while she was in nursing school and subbed as an occasional caregiver for his aging father. He'd been very supportive when her parents died and told her more than once since that if she ever needed anything, she should call him. Hannah had never taken him up on his offer until now.

She took a chair in the waiting room, still panting a little from her shortcut up the stairs, and tried to calm her red curls by running her fingers through them. As she did so, the reception room door opened and the tall, attractive man from the Mercedes and the elderly woman in the wheelchair entered. The old woman fixed her eyes on each of Dr. Harvey's patients in turn, seeming to x-ray them with her clear blue gaze. This woman might be elderly, Hannah thought, but she had all her wits about her. Energy and intelligence fairly radiated from her.

The older woman wore expensive clothing appropriate for this chilly March day in Denver—a wool and cashmere coat, fur-lined leather boots and a silk shawl around her shoulders that probably cost as much as Hannah's entire outfit. Every hair was in place and her makeup was expertly applied. She could have been anywhere between seventy-five and ninety, Hannah thought, because although she was frail and in a wheelchair, she looked both youthful and old at once.

Hannah returned her attention to the man pushing the wheelchair. When he laughed at something the receptionist said, his smile flashed white and even. She hadn't been privy to that smile in the parking lot, unfortunately. Still, the most noticeable things about him were the same remarkable blue eyes as those of his grandmother's.

He scanned the room for a place to sit. The only open spot was next to Hannah.

He didn't look any happier than she felt. "Do you mind if my grandmother sits here? There's a spot for her wheelchair."

"Please do." Hannah watched him as he patiently maneuvered the wheelchair into place and tenderly helped his grandmother remove her scarf and coat. In this throwaway society, some people behaved as if the elderly were dispensable, but not this man. He was irate over his car but, given the way he handled the older woman, Hannah could forgive him for that.

Settled, the old lady leaned toward Hannah, put her gnarled hand on Hannah's smooth one and whispered, "Don't mind him. You know how men are about their cars. He's been cranky lately. It's something about falling behind at work and needing to spend more time at his office. The car was just the straw that broke the camel's back. We'll have it fixed in no time."

Hannah wasn't sure it was that simple, but she smiled gratefully at the woman. "Thank you. I really am sorry."

The lady waved a dismissive hand and changed the subject. "This wheelchair is for the birds. I hope my broken foot heals quickly so I can get out of this thing. I drove my car until I was in my eighties, you know. Unfortunately, my doctor says I'm healing more slowly than I would have when I was younger."

Hannah looked toward the cast on the elderly woman's foot. "How did it happen?"

"I tripped on a Chihuahua, of all things! My friend brought her little dog with her when she came to visit. I'm not accustomed to having a dog around and it got tangled in my feet." Her laughter was like chiming bells. "Imagine that, ninety years old and tripped up by a dog smaller than my purse! My name is Lily, by the way. What's yours?"

Charmed, Hannah told Lily her first name.

"Oh, Hannah, you should have seen the fuss when I tripped on Wilbur! Imagine naming a dog Wilbur—whatever happened to names like Spot and Rover?" As Lily regaled Hannah with her dog incident, her grandson leaned back in his chair and wearily closed his eyes. He was asleep by the time his grandmother's name was called, Hannah knew, because his features had softened and the frown lines on his forehead were relaxed. He was even more striking in repose.

Without looking at Hannah, he jumped up and wheeled his grandmother toward the attending nurse. Lily waved goodbye to Hannah over her shoulder.

"I'll put you in room three," she heard the nurse tell them as they disappeared down the hallway toward one of Dr. Harvey's examining rooms.

Hannah picked up the daily paper on the table beside her, but her mind was focused on other things like Trisha's tuition, her eight-year-old son Danny's need for incidentals at school, not to mention heat, lights and food. Danny's jeans were already high-water and they were only a month old, a fact she considered a minor emergency. Kids at school had teased Danny about his too-short pants and her son had come home in tears. He also needed new shoes…again. What's more, Trisha had been right about Hannah's clothes, they were showing their age. Some of them were old enough to have cycled back into style again.

Then there was the mortgage she and Steve had taken out on the house. She remembered how giddy with happiness they'd been. Their first home—she'd loved it the moment she'd seen it. Small and cozy, it had two bedrooms on the first floor and a third under the eaves on the second. They'd remodeled the kitchen so it was sunny and bright. They'd drunk coffee at the small island every morning and discussed their plans for the day. She couldn't lose her house, not the one she and Steve had chosen together, the one in which she was raising her son. It was her last real physical connection to her late husband. Besides, where would they go?

She knew she shouldn't worry about her life—even what she would eat or drink—because it did no good. God already knew what she needed. Worrying couldn't add an hour to her lifespan, so why do it? That's what it said in Matthew 6.

Why had it become so difficult lately to trust this and to act on it?

The past seven years since her husband's death had tested her. Sometimes she feared she'd lost sight of God's plan for her. But, if fear was an avalanche, then God was the mountain. Here she was again, feeling fear sweep over her, blocking her vision of the future, even though she was rooted on the mountainous strength of God. Sadly, it was difficult to remember that when the surge was so wild and furious.

Dr. Harvey's nurse peeked out and beckoned her back to his office. "I'm squeezing you in," she said softly. "He can give you a couple minutes, but he's very busy so it might not be long."

"Anything is great. Thank you."

Dr. Harvey breezed into the room looking as fit as he had when Hannah had worked there. He was a little grayer, perhaps, but otherwise exactly the same.

"Hi, Hannah. It's good to see you." He shook her hand vigorously before dropping into his chair. "I have a patient waiting so I don't have much time, but I understand you are in a hurry to talk to me. My nurse used the word *panicked*."

"She was right," Hannah said ruefully and explained the situation. The more she spoke, the deeper the look of concern grew on the doctor's features.

When she was done, he grimaced. "I hate to tell you, but I don't have an opening and, frankly, don't know that many others do either. Budget cutting, belt tightening, you know what I mean. If I hear of anything, I'll make sure my nurse contacts you. Leave your information with me."

He appeared regretful as he added, "I'm sorry, Hannah. I really wanted to be more help than this."

She picked up her purse from the floor and smiled gamely at him. "I know. Thank you for taking the time to talk to me."

He opened the door for her. "Please, keep in touch. If I hear *anything*..."

She walked down the hall to the waiting room, shoulders squared, head high. She didn't want Dr. Harvey, who'd been so kind, to know the devastation she felt.

Tyler observed Dr. Harvey as he examined his grandmother's foot and studied the recent X-ray. His mind was only partially on the conversation between the other two. Why did that careless woman in the parking lot have to be so beautiful? With her cloud of red hair and delicate features, she was unique-looking. It was aggravating enough to have to repair the car—but it was worse that he couldn't get the one who did the damage out of his mind.

"How's the pain?" Harvey asked.

"Still there," Lily told him.

"You told me it was better," Tyler said with a frown. Lily had a way of not divulging things to him when she thought he might worry.

"It is, but it's *still there*." Lily pursed her

lips and cocked her head in the way she had when she was trying to charm someone. "I think my grandson is getting tired of taking care of me, doctor. Not that I blame him. I don't sleep much."

"Three to five hours a night is about it," Tyler felt tired just saying it.

"And I like his company," Lily added coyly.

"Four or more games of Scrabble every night."

Tyler could feel the doctor's appraising eyes on him. "You look exhausted."

Tyler didn't want to admit it, but the ninety-year-old woman was running him ragged.

"Have you considered live-in help?" Dr. Harvey asked. "Lily will be incapacitated for quite some time yet."

"They all quit for one reason or another." Tyler tipped his head slightly toward Lily to indicate the cause for the abdications.

"Oh, Tyler can take care of me. He's doing a wonderful job."

Tyler bit his lip to keep from disagreeing. He was mediocre, at best. And his business was suffering badly from his frequent absences.

"I know of someone who might help you. She worked for me while she was in school.

If we'd had any openings, I would have hired her myself. She's outstanding with the elderly. In fact, she even took care of my father for a time." Dr. Harvey copied a phone number onto the back of his business card. "Call her if you want. She's a widow with a young son. Her last name is St. James and she will do an excellent job for you."

Tyler politely took the card and put it in his coat pocket. He'd hired other excellent caregivers for Lily and she'd worn them out. Though Dr. Harvey was a good judge of character, should he hire someone to care for his grandmother on a single recommendation? Maybe he was so tired he was grasping at straws.

He was going to bring up the subject in the car on the way home, but before he could, Lily announced out of the clear blue, "I wish that lovely young woman we met in Dr. Harvey's office could help me, the one who ran into your car. She's a Christian, you know. I could tell. She wore a cross around her neck."

"A necklace isn't sure-fire proof of anything. Besides, she obviously can't drive. You'll need transportation to and from the clinic." Had the woman not been quite so lovely, Tyler might have objected to her more.

"I'm going to pray about it," Lily said firmly and closed her eyes as if to start immediately.

Lily's faith was rock-solid, Tyler knew. Living in Lily's orbit had taught him many things. If she wanted to pray, more power to her.

Despite what he'd said to Lily, he did need to consider the idea of calling the woman Dr. Harvey had suggested. If he didn't start paying more attention to his import and export business, it wouldn't exist much longer. He needed to be in the office daily. In and *awake,* that is.

Lily's eyes popped open and she said, "I'm thinking a little sunshine might be good for me. It would be nice if you closed up shop for a bit so we could go on a trip. Hawaii is always lovely." She squirmed in her seat. "It's just so *boring* with my foot in this cast."

A trip? Hadn't his grandmother heard a thing he'd said about falling behind at the office, that he needed to work more, not less?

Lily had just given him the reason to act. Tyler made up his mind. He would call the woman whose number was in his pocket as soon as he got home.

He'd simply keep her in line until he knew

she could do the job to his satisfaction. That had to be easier than taking Lily to Hawaii.

Besides, he had an escape clause—he could always fire the woman if Lily didn't run her off first.

Ty sat at his desk and stared out the window. Getting a good lead on someone to help Lily was a relief.

Lily hadn't sounded completely delighted by the prospect, but Tyler didn't care. Ever since they'd left the doctor's office yesterday, Lily had doggedly insisted that he go right out and find that "sweet young thing" who hit their car. Lily said that she was the only one she wanted to care for her. She even promised to try not to be difficult, if she could get her way in just this one thing. He'd believe that she could behave when he saw it.

Lily even liked the idea of having a little boy in the house when Ty told her the caretaker the doctor recommended had a child. She and Ty's grandfather had raised Ty from the time he was a small child. Ty's father had died not long after he was born and his mother never quite recovered from the shock. Adele Matthews had had a difficult time dealing with her own life. She had nothing left to give to a small child. That left Ty in his grandparents' care with a mother who flitted in and out of his life, until she'd passed away five years ago.

Lily went into a rhapsodic account of the wonderful times they'd had together when Ty was young. It would be just like "old times."

He couldn't argue with her. It was true. The whimsical, impulsive Lily and her indulgent husband were about as much fun to live with as any grandparents a child could have. They bought him a pony—Lily's idea—and taught him to golf in the backyard, at his grandfather's insistence. They'd also agreed Ty could eat ice cream for dinner for a week to see if he really could get sick of it (he didn't.) More amazing yet, Lily had let him keep a snake in a big fish tank in his room. His grandfather didn't even seem perturbed when it escaped and was lost for three days in the ductwork of the house. A maid discovered it, Ty recalled, right before she handed in her resignation.

Sometimes Ty thought he'd grown up to be more serious and mature than either of the adults in his life. At times he wished it weren't so, like now, when he spent so much time trying to please his grandmother.

Lily had already chased off several caretakers with her demands and she was *trying* to behave. Hannah would learn soon enough. *Whatever Lily wants, Lily gets.*

Chapter Two

"One thousand one, one thousand two, one thousand three…" Tyler was counting under this breath when he heard the tinkle of the small crystal bell. He'd given that wretched bell to his grandmother when he was twelve years old to commemorate her seventieth birthday. He'd never expected that twenty years later he'd be jumping to the sound of that same faint ringing that had once intrigued him.

With a sigh, he saved the document file and closed his computer. Then he put a smile on his face and walked across the hall to his grandmother's bedroom. He'd lost count of the times he'd done this tonight.

"Hey, there. What are you doing awake? It's after midnight."

"Oh, Tyler, I just can't sleep." Lily Matthews looked like a petulant child in her pink flannel nightgown. "I think it's that new medication I'm taking. Maybe some hot tea would help." She looked at him slyly through those bright and ageless eyes. "And a game of Scrabble. That always puts me to sleep."

"It does not. It winds you up like a clock. I have to go to work early in the morning, Grams. I can't be up half the night playing games." He was so tired already that his vision was blurring.

"Well," she huffed. "I'm sorry I'm such an *imposition*. Just the tea, then. I apologize for breaking my foot and becoming such a *burden* to you."

She was trying to guilt him into staying up half the night with her. He wouldn't fall for it this time, he told himself.

"I'm sure you didn't." He smiled a little. As much as his often manipulative, occasionally cantankerous grandmother drove him crazy sometimes, he loved her with all his heart. If only…

"…if only," she said, as if she'd read his mind, "that lovely woman you'd hired to help me hadn't left. Then you wouldn't have had to do everything for me. Did I ever tell you about the time…"

Lily Matthews was off and running. Tyler was too tired to listen.

The woman his grandmother was referring to hadn't *left,* exactly. It was more like she'd run away. Like the one before her. And the one before that. They'd all stayed a while, tending to his grandmother, hopping to her orders. Then they always resigned for the same reason—Lily was too much. She slept little, chatted constantly and was, although she'd never admit it, often imperious and demanding. She thought nothing of waking someone during the night to watch QVC with her or send her breakfast back to be remade two or three times because the poached eggs weren't quite to her liking. And taking her pills…that could be like World War III for a woman who was mentally somewhere in her thirties but trapped in the body of a ninety-year-old. Lily hated getting old.

She reminded him of a beautiful Ferrari with a purring engine whose wheels had been removed so the vehicle had been put up on blocks. Lily still had the engine but not the mobility.

It wasn't all Lily's fault, Tyler knew. His

grandfather had spoiled her outrageously over the years and had never once complained about her strong personality or over-the-top demands. Lily was behaving just like she always had.

The difference was that Ty was not his grandfather. He didn't have a staff of servants or a business manager and a massive team of people to run TDM Imports and Exports. After his grandfather had died and Ty had taken over his business, he'd trimmed much of the fat both personally and in the organization. Keeping it lean and trim had allowed him to be successful, even in the economic downturn. But he hadn't counted on Lily breaking her foot and insisting that she move into his house to be cared for. Nor had he expected her to demand that he bestow the attention on her that his grandfather once had.

Running the business, traveling and watching out for Lily, with no one but an infrequent home health care nurse and an occasional cleaning lady to help, wore him out. It didn't help that Lily was a night owl.

Still, he loved his grandmother. It was his turn now to take care of Lily. Honor your father and your mother—or your grandmother—had become his mantra, the thing he told himself when Lily was particularly irascible. It was all about her frustration at being unable to be as active as she once had, he reminded himself.

When he returned to his grandmother with the tea, she'd already dumped the Scrabble tiles onto the small table in front of her and she gave him that *surely you don't mean to deny me* look. She took the cup, tasted it and smiled sadly. "Just a little warmer, dear. Do you mind terribly?"

Warmer, colder, higher, lower, deeper, wider. It was always something with Lily. A wave of tiredness spread through him. It was going to be another of those short, short nights of sleep. He would call the number Dr. Harvey had given him first thing in the morning. He'd ask the woman if she could start tomorrow.

Chapter Three

Hannah pulled into the circular drive in front of the massive two-story brick home. As she did so, the butterflies in her stomach multiplied. This interview simply mattered too much. She was on the ropes and had no where else to go. Tyler Matthews had called her first thing this morning and she'd immediately agreed to a ten o'clock appointment with him.

"Lord," she whispered. "Please let this be the place."

She rang the bell and held her breath as the door swung open to reveal a dark cavern of rich cherrywood and parquet flooring. A round table that looked old and valuable sat in the center of the foyer with a flower arrangement on it that was at least four feet high, the kind she'd seen in the reception areas of fancy hotels. Those flowers alone would have paid her phone bill for six months.

She reached out her hand to the gentleman at the door and said, "Hello, I'm Hannah St. James. You called me to…" Then she looked into his face and a single word slipped out. "You!"

He stared back at her, obviously equally surprised. "From Dr. Harvey's parking lot? I had no idea…"

Of course not. There'd been no way to make such a connection. Dr. Harvey must have gone right into the next examination room and told these people about her. "Neither did I." He'd never let her take care of his grandmother after what she'd done to his brand-new car.

"I was there looking for work," she managed shakily.

"And he suggested we call you," Tyler said, seemingly staggered that she'd turned up on his doorstep.

A faint bell chimed upstairs and they both glanced in that direction.

"My grandmother. I'll be right back."

"I could come and say hello," Hannah

offered, hoping to revise his first impression of her.

"Not yet. My office is to the left. We have to talk first."

Feeling uncomfortable and tongue-tied, Hannah feared she wasn't making a very good impression. What's more, Matthews kept looking at her strangely as she sat at his desk in the chair across from him. Perhaps he expected her to do something silly... again. Still, there'd been a coffee service on the corner of the desk and he'd offered her a cup. The man had manners when one wasn't crashing into his fender.

"I need someone who is willing to move in and live here in this house," Tyler was saying.

"I can't, Mr. Matthews. I own a home. I live with my sister and eight-year-old son. It wouldn't be right to leave them."

"No husband then?"

The next words out of his mouth startled her so that her jaw dropped.

"Bring your son along. He can live here with you. Your sister, too, if you like. My grandmother enjoys children. They could entertain each other."

"My sister is in college. She's old enough

to live on her own, but Danny...you'd really permit that?"

Tyler sat back in his chair and crossed his arms over his broad chest. "Here's the deal, Mrs. St. James."

"Hannah."

"Very well, Hannah. My grandmother is a spitfire. She has energy that some forty-year-olds don't have. She's not accustomed to being confined to a wheelchair and the lack of mobility makes her irritable. I have an import and export business that needs my immediate attention. I love my grandmother with all my heart, but I can't make her happy and still run my business. I need someone to live in the house, be available to her 24/7 and to keep her busy. It isn't an easy job. Frankly, I'm getting desperate."

So desperate that he'd hire even her? Was that why he hadn't turned her away at the door when he recognized her?

"That's asking a lot."

"You'll have your freedom and time off, but you'll need to work around my schedule. I want someone here for Grams if she gets into mischief. Grandmother doesn't normally *get* into trouble, of course. She usually *creates* it."

She studied him closely. He looked tired. Huge stacks of papers and files littered his desk. What's more, she understood what he was saying about his grandmother. As people aged, their hours passed more slowly, and they craved contact with others and ways to fill those empty spaces. Lily would probably prefer that Tyler never leave her side at all except to sleep—and then for as few hours a night as possible.

"Frankly, Mr. Matthews, I'm surprised you're even talking to me. After all, I'm the one who ran into your new car. You must think I'm irresponsible, yet you're willing to hire me?"

His eyebrows rose and his blue eyes widened. A smile crept across his face. "Frantic is what I am. I wouldn't let you drive Lily to the clinic, but if you stayed inside the house…"

Hannah couldn't help smiling. If he could make a joke of it, so could she.

"There is one rather large problem, however."

Her heart sank a little. "Oh?"

"Yes. I'd like you to start immediately. You can move in this evening. I realize you'll have to go home and pack. Maybe you can bring what you need for the week and then take your time getting the rest."

He was asking her to leave her home, move in with virtual strangers and raise her son in an unfamiliar place—all in a matter of hours? It didn't even sound rational. Was the Matthews home in a different school district? She didn't know. She didn't have gas money to be driving Danny back and forth to school.

"I need time to think."

"I'm afraid I need an answer now."

Hannah opened her mouth to protest, but instead "I'll take it" popped out.

"Good. I want to let Lily know you're here before she sees you. Then I'll show you the house."

He left Hannah in his office while he mounted the stairs to Lily's room.

She was sitting in her rocking chair, knitting. Her white hair was a tumble of tight curls. She looked practically angelic in her pale pink velour outfit.

Looks could be deceiving, Ty thought wearily.

"You didn't bring her up to meet me."

"You *have* met her. She's the woman who ran into us at the clinic."

"With that dreadful little car? That sweet thing? Scoop her up."

When Ty paused, Lily's jaw hardened and her eyes turned flinty. "I liked that girl. If you can't get her, then just toss me into the nursing home so you can tend to your business and get me completely out of your hair. Maybe I should just check myself in."

Lily always threatened to check herself into some institution or another when things weren't going her way. Ty's grandfather had always considered Lily's occasional petulance cute and bent over backward to fulfill his wife's wishes. It had given him great pleasure, in fact, to spoil his Lily.

Tyler wasn't like his grandfather, but he didn't like to cross Lily any more than the older man had.

"I did hire her, Gram. I'll bring her up. She has to go home to pack a few things, of course, but she'll be back tonight."

Lily's face was suddenly wreathed with smiles. She reached out and patted his hand. "Darling boy."

She looked so pleased that Ty couldn't feel

too badly about doing something so impulsive. He wanted only the best for his grandmother.

Lily had become forgetful lately. Dr. Harvey had casually said that it was likely a result of being upset about her fall and that he doubted that it was the early stages of dementia. *Dementia.* Ty had never before considered such a thing happening to Lily. It changed how he thought about his grandmother. Since that conversation, Ty had feared the worst and hoped for the best.

That's when he'd decided that whatever Lily wanted, Lily would get.

"You'll have the room next to Lily's," Tyler told Hannah as he began his tour of the house. "She insisted upon it. There's a dressing room and bath between the two rooms, so you can use the adjoining door to get into her room if she needs you at night. If she isn't feeling well, you might want to leave both doors open so you can hear her. Otherwise, there are monitors in each room you can turn on at night."

His proximity was unnerving her. His cologne was crisp and masculine combined with the sharp sweet scent of soap. She closed her eyes for a moment, enjoying the experience.

Her eyes sprung open. Enough of *that!*

"Is she a restless sleeper?" she inquired, switching her thoughts from him to his grandmother.

"Not once you convince her to go to sleep. It usually takes me several games of Scrabble and begging for mercy before she agrees to go to bed." He paused on the landing between the stairs that led to the second floor. "Lily's a handful, Hannah. Like I've said before, my grandfather doted on her. He felt it was his purpose in life. She's not accustomed to not having her own way."

"We'll be fine. I like a challenge," Hannah said bravely.

"Then you should have a great deal of fun with my grandmother."

Hannah's new room was filled with sunshine. It had pale yellow walls, soft yellow sheers on the windows, a white coverlet decorated with yellow flowers and accents the color of tender green shoots peeking from the ground in early spring. It was larger than she'd expected, with room for not only the queen-size canopied bed, but also a love seat and chair, a desk and a small entertainment center hidden inside an armoire. The bathroom was equally pleasant with white subway tile, a claw-footed tub and a mirrored vanity for putting on makeup.

"This is lovely," Hannah said softly. She was touched that he'd chosen such a room for her.

"It's one of the larger bedrooms. I'm afraid that Danny's room is quite a bit smaller."

"Danny? He can stay in here with me. All we need is a cot or mattress."

"Lily wouldn't hear of that. Come. I'll show you his room. Then you can say hello to Lily."

She followed him down the hall to a room that was surely a little boy's dream. Painted balsa wood airplanes of all types hung from the ceiling, flying over a double bed. In one corner was a foosball table and in another a towering stack of plastic bins filled with Lego.

"Danny will stay here? This looks like it was put together just for him."

"It was, in a way."

She cocked her head to look at him.

"This was my bedroom when I was Danny's age. I put every one of those airplane kits together and convinced my grandfather to hang them. He liked Lego as much as I did, so we rarely went shopping without coming home with another kit. Danny can build the Capitol Building here in Denver, the Denver Art Museum and probably the U.S. Air Force Academy in Colorado Springs with all those."

Hannah sat down on the bed and put her hands to her mouth.

"What's wrong? Do you want him to have a television? I suppose I could…"

"No, of course not. I'm just astounded at how perfect this suits us. Danny will be over the moon! God is good." Tears stung at the backs of her eyes. She hadn't realized just how tense she'd been until this moment. She hadn't trusted God nearly enough.

He studied her but said nothing.

She wasn't acting the way he'd anticipated. He wasn't sure what it was he had expected, but it wasn't this. She looked about to burst into tears. Lily had said the little boy would enjoy his old room, but this?

What made Hannah St. James tick? He'd assumed that Lily would chase her off even faster than she'd run off the others, but now he was beginning to wonder. Maybe it wouldn't happen that way. Hannah seemed more desperate for a job than the others he'd hired. That vulnerability brought out feelings in him that he hadn't felt for anyone but his family. He shook it off, chalking it up to exhaustion.

"Do you want to say hello to Grandmother?"

She wiped away a tear that had slipped onto her cheek and stood up. "Yes, of course. Excuse me for getting teary-eyed. My son will love this. He's such a good little boy and I haven't always been able to give him all I'd like. I'm happy that he'll be able to stay in this wonderful room while we're away from home. Danny has been my best buddy since his dad died and I can hardly wait to see his face when he sees these airplanes."

Being a jobless widow was certainly enough to explain her desperation for a job and her determination to see it through. Maybe she would be the one who'd stick it out.

Lily was waiting for them.

"Finally! I thought you were never going to bring her to me, Ty." Lily clapped her hands together with obvious glee. "We're going to have such fun!"

"Fun? She's here to take care of you, Gram, not play games."

"My foot is broken, not my sense of humor. Don't be a rain cloud, Ty, darling. Those other women you hired were kind but such duds. I can tell already that Hannah will be a live wire compared to them."

He glanced at Hannah, who was staring at Lily wide-eyed. It was probably just sinking in, all that he'd told her about his grandmother's unquenchable energy and unreasonable demands. He hid a smile. *Poor Hannah.* Only she didn't know it yet.

Hannah moved close to Lily and took her hand. "We will have fun, won't we? My son Danny is going to love you. Thank you for allowing me to bring him to your home."

"I love little boys. I raised Ty, you know. He was a dream child. I can hardly wait to meet your son."

"Then I'd better go home and start packing."

When Ty turned to look at Lily, she was beaming like a lighthouse.

Chapter Four

The next few hours was a flurry of throwing clothing, personal items and other bare necessities into suitcases. She'd have to return later to get the rest. As she packed, it occurred to Hannah that she'd thrown very little away in the past seven years. She had clothes that she knew she would never wear again, but Steve had liked them.

She'd heard Trisha come in earlier and decided to go tell her the news about her job. Hannah was at Trisha's door before she realized her sister hadn't heard her in the hall. Had Trisha known, she probably would have cut short the phone conversation she was having. Her voice was clear as it carried through the half-closed door.

"It's the only thing I can do, Emma." Trisha's

voice was firm as she spoke on the phone. "I have to drop out of school after this semester. I know my sister says I shouldn't, but that's what she always says. If I'm not in school, I can get a full-time job instead of the little part-time thing I have. Besides, I'm sick of having no money to spend. I'm young. I want to have some fun even if my sister doesn't seem to remember what fun is."

Hannah cleared her throat.

"Listen, Emma, gotta go. Why don't you and Jane come over here?" She turned to her sister. "Did you hear that?"

"I heard enough. You can't mean what you said."

The younger woman's dark eyes flashed. "I totally mean it. I know I've never had a 'real' job or a handle on money but…"

"You have never been a burden to me, Trisha. I am so proud of you that I can hardly stand it. You only have three semesters to go. You can't quit now or you'll waste all that time you spent *and* my money. I won't have it."

"I'm taking this decision out of your hands, Hannah. I've made up my mind. Your agency couldn't make it. How are you going to find work when Family Affairs couldn't find it for you?

"You've cared for Danny and me all alone ever since Steve died. You've paid the mortgage, raised the two of us and sacrificed everything so that we'd be okay. If I had extra money, the first thing I'd do is buy you a new wardrobe. You have a dynamite figure. With your amazing hazel eyes and beautiful auburn hair, you could be gorgeous, sis."

"No, thank you. And my clothes are fine." Instinctively, Hannah glanced in the dresser mirror.

The woman who looked back had her long curls pulled back in a clip because she'd skipped haircuts the past few months. She wore clothes that had once been attractive but were now hanging loosely on her frame. She could have used a little more makeup, too, blush especially, to counteract her pale cheeks.

"I have news that might change your mind."

Trisha stared at her skeptically. "I doubt it."

"I took a job today."

Shock registered on Trisha's face.

"I'll be caring for an elderly woman who fell and broke her foot. She's a delight. I'm *very fortunate* to get this position. It means that there's no need for you to quit school."

"What's the catch?" Trisha narrowed her eyes. "There has to be one. I thought there weren't any jobs out there."

Hannah took a deep breath. "I have to start today. And I've agreed to move into their home to care for this woman."

"Move? What about Danny? What about *me?*"

The doorbell rang and she heard the front door open before she could comment. Emma and Jane, no doubt.

The girls had grown up together, attended grade school, high school and now college together. Sometimes they could finish each other's sentences and often found themselves shopping separately but purchasing exactly the same outfits.

"What's up?" Emma inquired. "You guys look serious."

"My sister found a new job," Trisha said.

"Congratulations!" Jane turned to Trisha. "Now you can stay in school."

"Sometimes I think you'd do just about anything for me and Danny, Han. I don't know about this. It's awfully sudden."

"I'll have you know that this is a very good

job. The pay will actually be higher than I was getting through the agency because they won't be taking their fees out first. It's caring for an elderly woman with a broken foot. She's cute as she can be and very interesting. I think we'll enjoy each other."

"But you'll be moving! That's huge."

"Move out of here?" Jane looked shocked, as if Hannah had announced that they were losing their home.

"It's just temporary, girls. I plan to take Danny with me. Trisha will continue to stay here. I'd be paying on this house anyway, whether Danny and I are here or not."

She studied the girls appraisingly. "Trisha told me that you two are planning to move out of the dorm to get a place of you own. Maybe you could move in here for a while and take your time finding a place. By the time I want to move back in, you will have found something you really like."

"You mean we could live here?" Jane turned hopeful eyes to Hannah. "We'll pay rent, just like we would if we were renting anywhere else."

"Plus, this place is nicer than anything we could find. And we'd be with Trisha," Emma pointed out. "We've always wanted to room together, but, of course, Trisha has had to live at home."

Now it was Hannah's turn to gape. With barely a blink, her problem had been solved. She loved these friends of Trisha's. They were Christian, well-mannered and responsible—her dream renters. And Trisha wore an expression of pure joy. Hannah hadn't realized until that moment how much her sister had missed not being able to do some of the things her friends had done.

The girls jumped to their feet and hurried upstairs, probably to decide how to divvy up the bedrooms.

Hannah continued to sit at the table and allow the wonderment to wash over her. Wasn't this just like God? Solving problems in the most unexpected ways?

Praise You, Lord, and thank You.

Now she could quit worrying about Trisha and the house. The mortgage wouldn't be a problem once the girls' rent started coming in.

"I look like I'm moving out for years," Hannah said wryly as Trisha carried her duffel bag into the entry and put it with the suitcases piled there. "How busy can one little old lady keep you?" Trisha asked.

Hannah thought about Lily's sparkling eyes and determination. "She's nearly run her grandson into the ground. I'm not sure she'll be any easier on me."

"About this guy who hired you," Trisha began, "what's he like?"

"I admire the concern he has for his grandmother," Hannah said vaguely. "He's kind and compassionate with her." The fact was, she didn't know much about him at all.

"Which reminds me, while I'm gone don't forget that you're in charge of writing checks to pay the mortgage and utilities. I put your name on the account along with mine. It's time you started taking on some financial tasks around here." Sometimes Hannah worried that she, by shouldering so much responsibility, had deprived her sister of valuable experience in running a household. "The bill from the garage for fixing my car should come soon, too."

"Sure. No problem. Should I start carrying your things to the car?"

"Didn't I tell you?" Hannah said as she sorted through books on the bookshelf in the entry. She grabbed a few she'd been meaning to read and put them in a large tote. "Mr. Matthews is coming to pick these things up."

"Whoa, a real gentleman!"

Hannah glanced out the window. Tyler Matthews, his dark hair ruffled by the breeze, was getting out of a Land Rover so shiny and black it looked as if it were made of patent leather. He wore jeans and a pale blue golf shirt that did nothing to hide his muscled chest and well-developed biceps.

"I see he's here to pick up my things now."

"*He's* your new employer?" Trisha gasped when she looked out the window. "No wonder you took the job! If I were you, I wouldn't move back home at all. He's gorgeous! You haven't dated in forever. Maybe…"

"Erase that from your mind right now," Hannah ordered sternly. "Do you think I'm so unprofessional that I'd even consider such a thing? Tyler isn't interested in me. It's Lily he's concerned about, and his business, which he's been neglecting. I'm a means to an end for him and vice versa. He'll get to tend to his business and I'll get you through school and that's it."

Trisha picked up a sweatshirt with puppies on the front that Hannah had laid on a chair and held it up. "When did you turn into a stodgy old lady, Hannah? You're beautiful, you're funny and you're smart. Get rid of the puppies. Put on a little makeup and kick up your heels. That's what I'd do."

Hannah had no doubt of that and it concerned her a little.

"If my heels leave the ground, I'll fall onto my face."

"Suit yourself," Trisha said with a sigh. "But for the record, I think you're crazy…"

The doorbell rang.

"…to pass *that* up without a fight!"

Hannah gave her sister a dirty look and opened the door.

Tyler did look good, standing there in the sunlight, no doubt of that. He flashed her a relaxed smile. "Ready to go? My grandmother is chomping at the bit to have you come."

Hannah stepped aside to reveal the stack of suitcases. "Ready as I'll ever be except that I haven't told my son yet. Danny went to a friend's house after school. He's going to have a big surprise waiting for him."

Suddenly, Trisha brushed by her, hand out. "Hi, I'm Hannah's sister, Trisha."

"Nice to meet you." Tyler smiled at the girl

and Hannah could see her sister melt. "Thanks for being willing to share her with me."

"Anytime. She's all yours." The way Trisha said it made Hannah want to blush.

"We'd better get going." Hannah picked up a suitcase.

Tyler took it out of her hand, grabbed another bag and took them to the vehicle, where he tossed them in as if they were featherlight.

"You can follow me." Ty slid into the Land Rover.

Hannah turned to Trisha. "I'll be back to pick up Danny when his friend's mother drops him off."

"I want to see the house this hunk comes from," Trisha said wistfully.

Hannah smiled and intentionally stepped on Trisha's toe.

"You can't stop me, Hannah," Trisha whispered. "This is the guy for you." She backed up quickly before she could get stepped on again. "Mark my words."

This is the guy for you. Hannah was surprised at the shiver of anticipation that statement produced in her.

"Your sister seems nice," Ty commented

as they drove away. "She looks a little like you but she's not a redhead."

"Trisha and I are very different. I suppose some of that comes from being more like a mother than a sister to her."

"You've taken a lot on those not-so-big shoulders of yours."

Hannah smiled at the oblique reference to her size. "Believe me, I've wished they were bigger many times, but it's forced me to turn the load over to God." She wasn't sure how that statement would go over with him. She had no ideas of his faith or values.

She glanced at him. He was smiling softly, just as he did for his grandmother.

"You sound like Gram."

The way he said it made her feel like she'd received a stamp of approval. Her shoulders sagged in relief.

Still, by the time they got to the Matthews mansion, Hannah had a roaring headache. She had enough anxiety about this job without Trisha's ridiculous comments, which continued to niggle at the back of her mind.

At least there was one down and only one to go, Hannah thought. Danny loved their house. Like her, it was his only tangible connection to his father. It had been easier than she'd expected with Trisha, but her son might not embrace the change quite so readily.

There was another hurdle too, she thought, a high one—making Tyler Matthews' home her own.

When Hannah returned to get Danny, he greeted her at the front door fresh from the shower. His slicked-back blond hair was tamed for the moment, except for his determined cowlick, which stood straight up. Danny was the real-life version of Dennis the Menace in both looks and actions. He was also a chip off the old block where his father was concerned. Steve's childhood pictures and Danny's were so similar as to be interchangeable.

"Hey, Mom." He ran into her arms and she hugged him so long that he squirmed away. "What can I have for a snack? Potato chips?"

"Take an apple."

"Borrrring." He shuffled off, hands in his pockets, cowlick pointing at the ceiling.

"Wash your hands first."

Danny waved them in the direction of the running water, pretended to dry them on a towel and dived for the cookies.

"I have something to tell you."

"You got a job already?"

"I did, but it's going to be a little different for us than my other jobs have been."

"Different how?" Mistrust fairly glowed on his features. Danny was wary of change.

"I'll be caring for an elderly woman. She lives with her grandson, who travels and is very busy with his business. He wants me—us—to move into his house, so that when he is away, his grandmother won't be alone."

"We're moving?" Danny gasped.

"We'll only be there a few weeks. The lady has a broken foot, which should heal nicely. Trisha will stay here. Emma and Jane are going to live with her. You and I will be at the new house as long as I'm needed."

"Can I go to my same school?"

"Yes, I checked."

"Will I have my own room?" He stuffed two cookies into his mouth. "Where's it at?" He sputtered crumbs as he talked.

At least he wasn't fighting her on this, kicking and screaming.

"In Cherry Hills Village, where they just built the new dog park last year. Your daddy used to golf at the country club there when he was young."

"The dog park?" His eyes grew wide. "You mean the one by Josh's house?"

Hannah had transported the boys back and forth for play dates occasionally. Josh's home was in a posh neighborhood not far from that area. "Yes, I believe so."

"You mean Josh and I will be *neighbors?*"

Hannah watched as her son's expression turned from doubt to elation. "That's cool! When are we going? I better call Josh, and I need to pack." He shot out of the room like a bullet out of a rifle.

Overcome, Hannah put her head into her hands and whispered, "Thank You, thank You, thank You, Lord. You are breaking down the barriers and paving the way. Please help me not to disappoint anyone now." She felt dampness on her cheeks as her tears began to fall. The tension that had been building within her melted away; the strain that had been wearing at her was gone and she felt release.

Trisha came home to change clothes and then announced, "I'd better get going. I promised Emma and Jane I'd meet them at the house before dinner to help them move in."

"That didn't take long."

"We're so excited to be living together. I've wanted this for a long time."

"Just remember, it's only until Lily Matthews is back on her feet."

"I know, I know, but it will be fun."

"Don't have so much fun that you forget to pay the bills," Hannah warned.

"Han, I'm a big girl. Honestly, you're treating me like a child!" Trisha stormed out and Hannah heard the front door slam shut.

Hannah and Danny pulled into Ty's driveway a few hours later, and Hannah began taking Danny's luggage out of the car. It felt like he had packed his rock collection the bags were so heavy.

Ty walked up beside her and extended his hand. "May I take that for you?" He reached for the suitcase.

Before he could say more, Danny pulled on his trouser leg.

"I'm Danny," he said and thrust out his hand. "Are you the man we're going to live with?"

Chapter Five

It was love at first sight.

When Danny walked into Lily's room, she chortled with delight. Danny, who was accustomed to spending time with adults, fearlessly sauntered directly to her. "I'm Danny," he announced. "Who are you?"

"I'm Lily Matthews," the old lady said, beaming. "But you may call me Gram."

"Okay, Gram."

"Have you seen your new room yet?"

Danny shook his head emphatically. "Nope."

"Hannah, wheel me down to Danny's room," Lily said imperiously. "I want to show it to him myself."

Hannah felt a little like saluting, but she restrained herself.

Lily immediately began regaling Danny

with stories from Ty's childhood. "He drew airplanes all over one wall with my lipstick… liked to sneak out his window at night and sleep with the dog in the garage…lived on peanut butter and bananas one entire summer…"

When they reached the door of Danny's new room, Lily said, "He can push me back to my room when we're done. You two run along now. Danny and I have things to talk about."

It was as if she'd lost interest in Hannah and Tyler. For Lily, the only ones left in the world were her and Danny. They already had their heads together, giggling over something.

"That didn't take long," Tyler commented when they reached the kitchen.

"Danny likes older people. The neighbors on both sides of our house are elderly and they've all taken him under their wings since his dad died. He's very comfortable with people over eighty."

"Obviously. Coffee?" Tyler gestured toward a pot on a warmer.

"Sure." Hannah wasn't sure how to behave. Tyler held the next few weeks of her life in his hands. Thankfully this was much easier than she'd expected. Despite their bad start, he was now completely gracious—and gorgeous, just like Trisha had said.

"Sit down." He poured coffee into two mugs and set them on the table. Then he brought a small pitcher of cream out of the refrigerator. "Sorry, no cookies. I haven't had time to stop at the bakery."

"If I have time, I can bake a few. Lily might enjoy sitting in the kitchen while I do it. Surely staying in her room all the time gets boring."

"I'm sure she'll let you know." He sank into a chair across from Hannah.

"You're tired, aren't you?" she blurted, forgetting herself.

He scraped his fingers through his dark hair, leaving it pleasingly rumpled. "That's an understatement. I'm exhausted. I'm not cut out for three or four hours of sleep a night, but that's what it has been." He studied her thoughtfully. "Lily is both lovely and a lioness, Hannah."

"You're not very optimistic about this. You think I can't handle it."

"Let's just say that some highly experienced caregivers have resigned."

"I'll make it work." She wrapped both

hands around the coffee mug and stared into its depths. *I have to!*

Danny providentially entered the kitchen at that moment. "Lily said that if I came down here I could have hot chocolate. Is that right?"

"Oh, honey, we can't—"

"Sure." Ty got up. "I'll show you where things are and you can make it yourself from now on."

"Cool." Danny followed Ty from the refrigerator to the silverware drawer to the cupboard like a shadow.

He hadn't been around many men. Hannah hadn't really dated anyone since Steven died and though Trisha had occasional boyfriends, there were none serious enough to bring home. One of the elderly neighbors played chess with Danny and another taught him about World War II and helped him put airplane kits together, but that was the extent of his adult male companions. She feared that it might be part of the reason that Danny was so vulnerable to the bigger boys at school, who occasionally taunted him. Watching her little boy glue himself to Ty Matthews, she realized how much Danny must have missed that father-son, man-to-man contact. She liked the idea that, for a brief while at least, Danny would have a little of that in this household.

"You can take the cup outside," Ty told Danny as he opened the patio door that led to the backyard. "There are koi in the pond. Do you like fish?"

"You bet!" And Danny disappeared into the sunlight.

"Cute kid. He'll probably do a lot to improve Lily's mood. She really is partial to little boys."

"Thanks to you?"

"Can I help it that I was an adorable kid?"

She observed his blue eyes twinkle. In her book, he was still pretty adorable.

At that moment a woman of about sixty-five stormed into the kitchen. Faded brown hair haloed her face and her pale blue eyes flashed with electric fire. "I quit!"

"Not again," Ty said wearily. "What has she done this time?"

"She accused me of not cleaning her room properly. Dust on the sills or some such nonsense. And she blamed me for dust on the wings of those airplanes in your old bedroom! I cleaned that room three days ago. That dust has to be in her imagination. I've put up with your grandmother for twenty years, but no more. I'll gather my things. You can send my final paycheck. You know the address."

"Hannah, this is Irene. Irene has worked for us since I was in high school." He looked at the woman with sympathy. "And she can't quit now. I don't know what I'd do without her."

"You can't talk me out of it this time, sir. Being accused of not knowing how to clean? Well, I never!"

"Hannah will be here to help you now, Irene. She'll be in charge of my grandmother. That should take some pressure off you."

"Uh-uh. No, siree. I love your grandmother like a sister, but sometimes I don't like her very much. Demanding, domineering, bossy. It takes a saint to put up with her!"

"Aren't you about due for a raise, Irene?" Ty said, resignation in his voice. "A rather large raise?"

That stopped the woman for a moment. Then she shook her head. "You'd be better off finding someone younger, sir. Someone whose patience isn't stretched thin."

"I'll help you, Irene," Hannah blurted. "I'll be your go-between if you need a break. I don't mind—really, I don't. I'm used to working with older people. I'd love it if you'd stay."

The older woman eyed her as if she'd just lost her mind. "You're new. You have no idea what you're volunteering for. Pick, pick, pick, that's what Lily does. Nobody does anything quite right. She's sweet as pie while she's driving you insane. No, dearie, I couldn't do that to you."

"Give me two weeks to try. If I can't help you then…" Hannah held up her hands and shrugged.

"And the offer of a raise still stands," Ty jumped in. "Come on, Irene, it's a win-win for you."

She sighed. "If I didn't like you so well, Mr. Matthews…"

"You love my grandmother and you know it."

"We all do. But you're stuck and I'm not," she said, pointing out that Ty didn't have the luxury of quitting on his grandmother like she did.

"Two weeks. I'll give Hannah a raise, too."

Irene put her hands in the air. "Oh, all right. I'll go dust those windowsills and airplanes again."

After Irene had left, Hannah turned to stare at Tyler. "Does she quit often?"

"No. When she does, I know she's serious. Fortunately, I've always been able to talk her out of it. Irene keeps this place running. It would cave in on all of us without her." He stood up. "And now that I have staff, I'm going to the office." He took a camel-colored jacket off a hook by the door. "I'd better work fast, before you quit, too. See you at dinner."

She was left to stare after him. What on Earth had she gotten herself into?

Later that evening, she prepared to put her son to bed in his new room. Danny still smelled of soap and shampoo plus the old shaving lotion he'd found in a box in the attic and insisted on using. It had been his father's and the scent was nearly gone, but he found it comforting. So did Hannah. So little was left of Steve except for her son, her memories and her home. She'd loved him deeply. Now all that remained was a faint whiff of shaving lotion on her small son.

Lord, show me what's next. And please, can it not be so hard?

"Can I read to you tonight, Mom?" Danny had a book on rockets and outer space in his hand. "Did you know they retired the space shuttles in 2011? One of them is at the Smithsonian. Can we see it someday?"

"Time will tell, sweetie."

"You always say that."

"Because it's always true."

"Did you tell my dad that when he was alive?"

Danny always asked about Steve. Every time he did, it sent a spear of sadness through Hannah. This sweet little boy needed a father. He'd been cheated out of his relationship, just like she'd been cheated out of hers.

They read together for a bit. When Danny's eyes began to droop, Hannah tucked him in, kissed him on the forehead and turned out the light. Whatever suffering had transpired after Danny's birth was worth it, she knew, to have this little boy in her life. But her child needed more male role models in a life that was overpopulated with women.

That night, as she lay in bed in her own new room second-guessing herself, Hannah thought back to the initial catalyst that had spurred all this.

Chapter Six

It was forty-two cents.

Days ago, when she'd shaken her wallet looking for coins, a toothpick wrapped in clear cellophane, a tattered stick of gum and four pennies had fallen out. The note from Danny's teacher, the one he'd brought home with such excitement in his eyes and anticipation on his small, freckled features, lay on the table.

The second-grade class at Wilder Elementary will be taking a field trip to the History Museum on Wednesday. The cost is five dollars per student. This includes entrance fees, lunch and one snack during the visit to the museum. Please send cash with your student and put his or her name on the envelope.

Thanks in advance, parents. We plan
to have a marvelous day!
Mrs. Boswell

A sick feeling had settled in Hannah's gut
as she looked once again for nonexistent
money in her purse. She'd dropped the bag to
the table and turned toward her living room
furniture. In moments, she'd dismantled the
couch and two chairs and was running her
flattened hand in the furniture's crevices,
looking for spare coins.

She recalled the front door opening and
closing behind her and Hannah felt a gust of
cold, late-March wind sweep into the house.
"Close the door, Trisha. You're letting the
heat out!"

"What heat?" Her sister had come into the
living room rubbing her still-mittened fingers
together. "It's freezing in here."

"I had to turn down the thermostat. Do you
have any idea how much our heating bill was
last month?"

"No, and I really don't want to."

"It's my fault we're living like this—paycheck to paycheck, barely getting by," Trisha
said miserably in a half whisper. "We're
wearing long johns and jackets to bed and

eating pork and beans and Ramen noodles at the end of every month. And it's all because of me."

"Nonsense," Hannah said briskly. "If you want to be helpful, tell me you have forty-two cents."

Trisha looked puzzled but had obediently dug into her pocket and retrieved a quarter and two dimes.

Hannah sighed with relief then and took the coins from her younger sister's hand. "Now Danny can go on the field trip tomorrow. I was forty-two cents short."

Trisha had flung herself onto the couch now stripped of its cushions. "I could get on full-time at the café and earn some real money. I'm sick of scrimping."

"We can get by until you graduate. Once you're earning a salary, everything will be fine." Hannah had been exhausted down to the marrow of her bones. Sometimes she wished Trisha were a little more mature. She always talked like she understood financial matters but she was still pretty weak in common sense in that area. Hannah hoped it wasn't a mistake, running her so quickly through the nursing program.

"No. It's too much."

"You can't do that, not after making it this far. It would break my heart."

Trisha's pretty face was troubled. "Sis, you've been taking care of me since I was fourteen years old. I can't believe you aren't sick of it by now."

Hannah recalled wrapping her arm around her and pulling her close. "You are my family. It's you and me, babe, remember?"

It had been that way ever since her parents had succumbed to carbon monoxide poisoning while vacationing with friends in a ski chalet in Montana.

"You didn't ask to raise a teenager. You got dumped on. That's all there is to it."

"No, you know better than that." At twenty-four, Hannah had already graduated from nursing school and was old enough to take responsibility for her young sister. They'd made a home, the two of them, and when Hannah had married Steven St. James and given birth to her son, Danny, it had seemed they finally had a perfect family. Perfect, that is, until Steve, a high school teacher, had had a brain aneurysm burst while he was playing basketball with some of his buddies in the church gymnasium.

Left responsible for both her sister and

her son, Hannah had worked all she could, tightened the proverbial belt, prayed hard and trusted God to carry her through. She would keep doing the same.

"What's up, Hannah?" Trisha had asked her.

"A little setback, that's all. We'll be fine."

That had set Trisha on alert. "Define *setback*."

"Things are slow all over. The agency had to let me go, but I'll find work soon. No matter how rough the economy, people need help caring for elderly family members."

"You got fired? Hannah, that's terrible!"

"I got laid off, okay? That sounds better."

"Don't equivocate. You're out of a job."

"Listen, honey, I've been a professional caregiver since the day I graduated from college. That's when Dr. Harvey hired me to help care for his ailing father, remember? Until recently, Family Affairs had a waiting list of clients who'd asked specifically for me. It's just that there have been fewer inquiries into professional home care since the recession. More and more people are choosing to care for parents or grandparents themselves because of the cost. There will be another job soon, Trisha."

Doubt had clouded Trisha's features. "I know, I know, God will provide. But what do we do in the meantime? Go on a bread-and-water diet?"

Hannah had tried to respond slowly, careful not to say anything that might jar something loose inside her, like the frail walls that were keeping her composure in check.

"If things pick up, Family Affairs will consider rehiring staff." She'd worked at Family Affairs ever since she had gone back to work after Steve's death.

Trisha had been about to speak, but she stopped when the front door again flew open.

"Hey, Trisha, did Mom tell you about the field trip our class is taking tomorrow? It's going to be awesome!" Danny kicked off his boots, shed his parka and dropped his Spiderman book bag on the floor. Then he threw himself onto the couch between his mother and his aunt. "Right, Mom?" His green eyes, so much like his father's, glowed as he looked up at his mother.

"Yes, terrific." Hannah's voice sounded oddly strangled in her ears.

He looked at her quizzically but didn't pursue it. Instead he took Trisha's hand. "Can

I have popcorn and hot chocolate for my snack?"

"Sure, little buddy. Let's go." Trisha had allowed herself to be led into the kitchen.

Hannah had waved them away, behaving as if what they'd been discussing was unimportant. But it *was* important. Their budget was figured down to the penny. That had already been underscored by her inability to provide her son with forty-two cents for a field trip. What would happen to them now that she was out of a job?

She groaned and pounded on her pillow.

She had received three nasty collection letters in the mail. Never before had she felt so shamed. Granted, she'd been late to pay her bills, but she'd been sure she'd have the money soon. She'd never had a bad-check notice in her life—until now. How had things fallen apart so quickly?

Because, of course, they'd been living from hand to mouth ever since Trisha had started school. Her sister had applied for scholarships, but none were forthcoming. She held her small job as a waitress, but her studies were demanding. Every penny Hannah earned went toward bills. They had no cushion left for an emergency of any sort. She'd become the working poor and it grieved her terribly. What would Steve have thought? He'd been a fanatic about paying bills on time. He would never have let them get into this fix, but what else could she have done? Now, she'd had to move into the Matthews' house and out of the house to save it.

In her new, still unfamiliar bedroom, Hannah fell asleep and dreamed that she and Danny were moving across a vast desert, all their worldly possessions strapped to the back of a cantankerous camel. Sandstorms came and went. Every oasis turned out to be a mirage and she awoke with her mouth parched. She didn't want to know what a dream expert might say about that.

In the quiet of his office the next morning, Tyler replayed the scene with Irene last night.

He had to give Hannah credit for averting disaster by offering her help. If Irene had left, he would have been in a world of hurt. It only underscored how important it was that this young, delicate woman could handle Lily. The odds were against her, considering Lily's track record.

He was sorry, too. He liked the feisty redhead. She was definitely the prettiest caregiver they'd had, but the delicacy of her looks belied the spine of steel she exhibited. He found himself wishing to see her outlast his grandmother's imperious demands. Time would tell, he decided. Until then he'd silently cheer Hannah on.

"Morning, sir," his secretary Melanie had greeted him when he'd arrived. She'd picked up a sheaf of papers. "Things to sign. You've also got a lot of phone calls to return. Several new manufacturers have contacted us recently looking for an export agent. Your attorney has been calling. He's looked over those documents we sent to him and he's found a couple irregularities he'd like corrected before you sign them. There's a new wholesaler in Spain who wants to talk to you, and those catalogue companies we contacted have sent their bids. Oh, yes, and one of the freight forwarders wants you to look at the new shipping rates before he books cargo space."

She drew a breath before continuing, but Ty held up his hand. "Don't tell me any more. Just give me the things that needs immediate attention. When I'm done with that, I'll take the stuff that should have been done last week." He scraped a hand through his hair.

"I'm sorry to flood you with this first thing."

"It's hardly your fault." He took the papers she handed him. "Don't put any calls through for a couple of hours—especially from Lily. She has got help at home now. I'm going to have to wean her from calling on me."

She looked at him with surprise. "Yes, sir."

Ty lost himself in work, and when he glanced at the clock it was already one in the afternoon. Because Melanie hadn't sent through any calls, he'd taken care of many of the tasks before him. He wondered how many times his grandmother had called and how irate she was that she hadn't been let through.

Melanie was back from lunch and opening mail. The office was surprisingly serene. She turned around when Ty entered and handed him a list of phone calls to return.

He glanced at the list. "I see you haven't listed my grandmother. How many times did she call?"

"None, sir."

"What?" He wasn't sure he'd heard her correctly.

"She didn't call at all."

"I wonder if something is wrong." Then he stopped himself. He'd hired Hannah St. James to keep Lily busy. She was obviously doing it. He shouldn't, like Lily's old saying went, look a gift horse in the mouth. Surely someone would contact him if anything was wrong.

"Order me some lunch and have it delivered, will you? As long as it's quiet I'd better keep working."

He wandered back into his office and sat down feeling strangely bereft. He'd been on edge ever since Lily got hurt and then, suddenly, he wasn't needed. It was exactly what he'd wanted, but it felt strange.

The empty feeling reminded him of all the things he'd passed up in order to live the life he had. Sometimes he wondered if he took Lily's care too seriously. But she was the mother that his own mother was unable to be. Lily had been a socialite until he'd come to live with her, and she'd turned her back on all of it to nurture him. He had done the same for Lily.

It really hadn't been that much of a sacrifice. After his fiancée Anita's death, he'd never planned to marry again anyway. He believed that the kind of love they'd had never struck twice. They'd had what his grandparents had experienced. They were soul mates, best friends. He'd lived his life not believing he'd ever meet another woman like Anita.

He still felt he was to blame for her death. Anita had gone to Paris in part because of him. She'd gone to buy her wedding dress. She and her maid of honor had planned their shopping excursion down to the last detail and were so excited they talked of nothing else. After they'd found a dress, they rented a car to tour the countryside. They'd planned to be gone a week. A farmer's truck stopped in the middle of the road with a flat tire, a quick turn of the steering wheel during which Anita lost control of the car and they would never return.

He hadn't felt good about her going, but she was so looking forward to it that he hadn't had the heart to say so. If only...if only what? He had forced her stay home? Everyone, including Anita's family and his grandparents, would have told him he was being ridiculous. So he'd let her go and she'd never come back.

Hannah, he realized, was the first woman since Anita who appealed to him on more than a professional level.

To change the track of his thoughts, Tyler picked up another pile on his to-do list and dug in.

A soft knock on the door made him look up. Melanie peeked around the door. "I'm leaving now. Is there anything else you'd like me to do before you go?"

"Already?" He looked at his wristwatch. Six o'clock? "How did that happen?"

"No calls from your grandmother, perhaps?"

"I hope the house hasn't gone up in flames," he said wryly. "I can't imagine how Lily's new caregiver kept her off the telephone."

"Sounds like you've got a winner."

He was surprised to be able to agree.

When he reached the house, it was gleaming with light, lamps on in nearly every room. As he walked from the garage into the kitchen he could hear music playing—old music. The tunes of first "A Tisket, A Tasket" and then "Over the Rainbow" came floating from the back of the house, garnished with peals of laughter.

Chapter Seven

Tyler eased open the door and looked inside. What he saw made his jaw drop.

Lily and Danny were ensconced at the kitchen table dropping cookie dough onto baking sheets lined with parchment paper as music poured out of the radio. Irene, who was usually gone by this time of day, was at the other end of the table polishing silver. Hannah, in a vast white apron that dwarfed her small figure, was stirring something in a large, steaming pot on the stove. The entire house smelled wonderful—baking cookies, spicy sausage and chalky silver cleaner— and brimmed with energy. The place had done a one-hundred-and-eighty-degree turn since yesterday. It felt like the home he'd known as a child—full of light, music and fun. How had Hannah managed that in a single day?

Lily barely had time to look up and greet him.

Danny waved a teaspoon in the air. "We're making oatmeal-chocolate-chip cookies. They're my mom's specialty."

"They're delicious," Irene agreed. "I've had three and ruined my supper."

Ty walked to the stove and bent over Hannah's shoulder to see a creamy white soup in the pot. He could smell the sweet-savory sausage, the aroma of the cookies in the oven and a hint of lavender, which was no doubt Hannah's perfume or bath powder. He didn't know which of the aromas he liked best. The lavender was particularly enticing.

He felt large and towering as he stood over Hannah. She was almost five feet five inches tall but very slim. Her wrist bones were slight and appeared fragile, her fingers long and slender. Her hazel eyes sparkled with fun. She'd pulled her rusty auburn hair back with a ribbon, but small tendrils had escaped and curled around her face in the steam.

Ty felt an odd twist in his gut, as if she was

another person he needed to protect, but he shook it off. Hannah was plenty tough. After all, she'd kept Lily out of his hair all day. As he stood by her, another emotion overtook him, one he'd least expected—romantic interest. He wanted to put his arms around her and bury his nose in that red cloud of hair.

Pulling back, he stammered, "When will we eat?"

"It's ready now. As soon as Lily and Danny finish dropping the cookies, I'll set the table." She turned around and her shoulder brushed against his. Ty stiffened at the light, pleasurable touch. She, however, didn't seem to notice.

"Irene, will you join us? I made plenty of soup and baked enough bread sticks to feed an army."

"Oh, I shouldn't. I usually don't…"

"Stay, Irene," Ty said, "unless you have to cook dinner for your husband."

"He's not home tonight. Bowling with his buddies."

"Good. Set a place for yourself."

The woman smiled broadly. Ty couldn't remember the last time Irene had really smiled. Hannah was making miracles.

* * *

Hannah felt a surge of cozy domesticity she hadn't experienced in a very long time, not since Steve had been alive. Granted, she cooked for Danny and Trisha, but Trisha often didn't come home until long after Danny had eaten. Hannah wasn't quite sure when they'd begun eating in shifts rather than sitting down at the table to eat as a family. It had happened gradually, she supposed, or she might have put a stop to it. Then again, a lot of things had gone by the wayside since Steve had died. It saddened her to think of it, but she pushed it to the back of her mind. She had people to care for right now. That would have to fulfill her need for more family.

Irene put away the silver and set the table. Danny filled glasses with ice and water. Lily folded napkins. Hannah handed Ty a plate of homemade breadsticks and began dishing up bowls of soup.

When they sat down, Danny immediately put his hands together and lowered his head.

"Would you say the blessings, dear?" Lily murmured, glowing with pleasure.

"Dear God," the child began, "thanks for my mom's good Italian soup. And thanks for this awesome place to live. And the airplanes on my ceiling and the Lego…"

"Amen," Hannah said, knowing that if she didn't intercede, Danny could find things to be grateful for till bedtime.

They lingered over coffee and cookies, chatting, until Danny yawned. Irene glanced at the clock on the wall. "Mercy, me! It's eight o'clock. I'd better go home or my hubby will beat me home from bowling." She turned and beamed at Hannah. "I haven't had such fun in a long time. Thank you for dinner."

"Anytime, Irene. I like to cook. I know you usually leave a meal for Lily, but I don't mind cooking." She glanced hesitantly at Ty. "If you don't mind, that is."

"Mind?" He looked pleased. "How could I mind? But you don't have to, Hannah. That wasn't part of the agreement."

"If I live here, I expect to feed Danny and myself. No use always doubling up on meals."

"I think it's a wonderful idea," Lily interrupted. "And Ty will see what a good cook you are."

What did that have to do with anything? Hannah wondered.

"The way to a man's heart is through his

stomach," Lily added. "Ty's grandfather always said so."

Quickly changing the subject, Hannah said, "Danny, go upstairs and take a shower and get into your pajamas. Irene, I'll clean up in the kitchen after I've gotten Lily settled upstairs. Thanks for your help."

"How did you get down the stairs, Gram?" Tyler asked.

"With a crutch on one side and Hannah on the other. She said I didn't need to be trapped in my room every day."

"Well, how about I do this to get you upstairs?" Tyler leaned over his grandmother and swept her into his arms. "Hannah can carry the crutch." In a moment, Lily was back in her room. Ty deposited her on the bed and left her with Hannah.

The elderly woman was exhausted from her day, Hannah realized. Lily, probably for the first time in years, was ready for bed by 9:00 p.m. Hannah said good-night and closed the door behind her.

In Danny's room, Hannah kissed her son good-night and listened to his prayers. Before she could ask her son how he liked it here, Danny volunteered, "This is a great place, isn't it? I wish we could live here all the time."

"And leave our house and Trisha?"

"This is a way nicer house. And someday Trisha will get married and move away. You said so yourself."

"But not anytime soon, probably."

"Why not? She's graduating next year."

That set Hannah back on her heels. It was true, but she hadn't wanted to think about it. She'd given so much of her life to her sister that the idea of Trisha moving away was almost unimaginable. Soon it would be just she and Danny, and then… A wave of loneliness washed over her. Danny would go to college and she'd be completely alone.

Steve had been the love of her life, her soul mate. She couldn't imagine a man she could love more. And if she couldn't have the type of affection and devotion she'd once known, she wouldn't marry again. She'd never allowed herself a spark of attraction to another man, unless she counted today.

Back in the kitchen, Hannah was surprised to find Ty at the sink rinsing dishes. "I can do that."

"So can I." He began to load the dishwasher. "I would have starved long ago if I didn't know my way around a kitchen."

"What's your specialty?" Hannah picked up a sponge and wiped crumbs off the table.

"Panini sandwiches. Pile everything I can find in the fridge on a piece of thick bread, squash it all together with another piece of bread, butter it and smash it in the panini maker. The Iron Chefs have nothing on me."

They cleaned the kitchen in companionable silence. Ty poured two cups of coffee and handed one to Hannah. "I think I'll have a couple more cookies before I go to bed." He glanced at his watch. "Which, by the way, will be at a decent time for a change."

"Lily was already half asleep when I left her room."

"She obviously needs much more activity than she's been getting." He studied her, his dark eyes hooded and unreadable. "You're good at what you do, aren't you?"

"I like to think so. I have a passion for the elderly." Hannah considered the fervor she felt to make the world a better place one aged client at a time. She believed God had created her for this task. *Honor your father and your mother*—and those of others. *Look after the widows in their distress.* Even with no living parents of her own, those words resonated in her heart.

"I think I'll hit the sack," Ty said with a yawn. "Lily may not go to bed this early again for a long time."

"Lily won't be a problem, I promise. Don't worry, I'll take care of you." It surprised Hannah to realize as she looked at Ty that she meant it with all her heart.

His head hit the pillow with Hannah's words echoing inside his skull. Lily was her charge now. He breathed a deep sigh of relief. This meant he could finally get some work done. He'd made a dent in paperwork today, but even that wasn't the most pressing thing he had to accomplish. He'd put off visiting numerous manufacturers and customers and had several messages from his accountants and attorneys to tend to.

Before his mind could spin off in the direction of business and keep him awake despite his respite from Lily, he tried to think of something else. But the images that came to mind were almost as distracting as the import/export business. Hannah St. James, crashing into his Mercedes, enthralling Lily, cooking dinner on his stove, warming his kitchen with food and laughter. Smelling of lavender and cookies. None of it was what he'd expected.

He flipped from his side to his back and stared at the ceiling. Having Hannah around made him think about Anita. He'd imagined many scenes like tonight, but with her, not Hannah. He'd believed they were a match made in heaven, one much like that of his grandparents, which happened only once in a lifetime. When she'd died five years ago, he'd never expected to have feelings like that for another woman again. That was, after all, why he'd plunged himself so deeply into the business. There was little room for grieving over what he'd lost.

Besides, he'd created the business he'd desired and it took most of his time and his thoughts to keep it running at this fast pace. He couldn't let anything get in the way right now. The attraction he felt for this new addition to their family would have to go on the back burner. For the time being, at least, he had to keep his nose to the grindstone no matter how appealing Hannah St. James might be.

The next morning he woke up at five-thirty feeling refreshed. It was the first time since

Lily had broken her foot that he'd felt he could have a run before work. Lily never got up early. How could she when she refused to go to sleep at night? Ty pulled on his running clothes and tread softly down the stairs. He usually took a path that started by the kitchen patio and circled most of the neighborhood. It was only three miles, but at least it got his blood pumping in the morning.

Ty was surprised to find Hannah already in the kitchen in navy sweats and a lime-green jacket. She was tying her running shoes and glanced up as he entered.

"I didn't expect anyone to be up." Pillow wrinkles were pressed into her cheek and her hair had been pulled back carelessly. She looked like a teenager with her rusty-red hair pulled tightly away from her face and her ponytail thrust through the back of a lime-green baseball cap. Tendrils slipped out to frame her makeup-free face.

"Neither did I." She was even more beautiful without artifice. Women wore makeup for other women, Ty had decided long ago. He loved her naturalness and lack of pretension.

"I usually try to run before I wake Danny up for school. After that the day usually gets away from me."

"Do you want to run with me this morning so you get to know the trails?" He pulled his own jacket from the closet. The weather had been good for Denver in late March, but a jacket was still a definite necessity.

"I'd like that. If I'm too slow for you, feel free to leave me behind. I'll find my way home. I always do."

They started out slowly, chatting about the weather and the landscape.

"Thank you for inviting me to run with you. It's nice. I've run alone for years, but I find it good to have a companion, at least on a new path," Hannah said.

"Anytime," Ty surprised himself by saying. He and Anita had run together often. He'd liked the feel of her by his side. It had been difficult to continue running after the funeral, but he'd forced himself. He, too, had felt alone on the trails for a long time. What's more, Ty was supremely aware of Hannah's small presence next to him. He was even more aware that he liked it.

Chapter Eight

The next few days passed quickly as she and Danny grew accustomed to the Matthews' household. She was late today in bringing Lily her breakfast tray. Lily liked to sleep in on Saturdays. The old woman was frowning when Hannah entered the room. Her phone was next to her on the bed.

"You don't look very happy this beautiful morning," Hannah observed. "Are you feeling okay?"

"It's not me—it's my friend Clara. Something is wrong." She barely glanced at her tray, on which Hannah had made sure to put a fresh flower in a bud vase.

"What's the problem?" Ty asked. He'd followed Hannah upstairs with a carafe of coffee and mugs. It was his custom to have coffee with his grandmother on Saturday mornings.

It pleased Hannah to know that she was freeing him up to work, but she was glad for his presence on the weekends. Lily *was* demanding. She reminded Hannah of Danny as a toddler—always wanting to be entertained, becoming easily bored and having a short attention span.

She hadn't heard much from Trisha, and Hannah didn't know whether to be grateful or concerned. She seemed to be having a good deal of fun with Emily and Jane but often sounded scattered and disorganized on the phone.

The only time Hannah had been to the house, Trisha had been out. The girls weren't pristine housekeepers, but the place was relatively neat. It was good for her sister to be on her own, Hannah told herself, and it was about time. She'd peeked in the rolltop desk for unpaid bills. It was messy, but she hadn't found anything to suggest Trisha wasn't on top of things. She was probably worrying unnecessarily.

Ty sat down in a recliner across from his grandmother and poured a cup of coffee. "Care to join us, Hannah?"

"Oh, I shouldn't."

"Of course you should!" Lily said emphatically. To do anything else, her tone implied, would be utterly impolite.

Ty smiled, she noticed, as he poured her a cup of coffee. A crease in one cheek looked suspiciously like a dimple. Hannah had always been a sucker for dimples. One more reason Ty Matthews was one of the most handsome men she'd ever met.

Hannah was developing more and more sympathy for him every day. He was a champ to have lasted this long with his imperious grandmother. Without even realizing it, Lily had had Hannah on her toes all day long every day.

When she was entertained, Lily was as charming and delightful a woman as Hannah had ever met. But when she was displeased, Hannah had feared a magazine or hairbrush might sail past her head.

Despite these fits of temper, Hannah loved Lily more every day. She was clever, funny and generous to a fault. And she adored Danny, who, as soon as he'd had his after-school snack, went directly to Lily's room to tell her about his day.

Hannah settled on a straight-back chair next to the recliner and Ty handed her a mug. When their fingers touched she felt his warmth. Something lurched within her. That simple motion was the type of thing she'd missed most about not having a man in her life—not the showy public gesture, but the tiny, cozy moments that no one else knew about.

"My grandmother and Clara were in school together when they were girls," Ty was saying. "They've kept in touch ever since. About six months ago, Clara moved back to Denver to live with her sister and nephew. She and Lily were able to renew the friendship."

"Such as it is," Lily snorted. "We never see each other in person. Poor thing. She'd been crying when I called her this morning. She tried to pretend she had a cold, but I don't think so. She's not telling me everything." Lily looked directly at Ty. "You'll have to go over there and see if she needs help. What if she's sick and hasn't been to a doctor?"

"She lives with her sister, doesn't she?"

"Her sister doesn't drive. They depend on Clara's nephew to take them wherever they need to go." Lily turned to Hannah. "Something's wrong, I tell you. I won't rest until I assure myself she's okay."

Hannah recognized that tone of voice. Lily would not be dissuaded.

"I baked two batches of cookies yesterday. Perhaps you'd like to send some over to your friend?" she said mildly.

Lily clapped her hands. "Excellent idea! No one will question why you've come if you're delivering something from me. You can go right now, Ty. Take Hannah with you. Both Danny and Irene are here. I'll be fine." She promptly shooed them away.

Out in the hall, Tyler asked, "Are you sure this is a good idea?"

"One, it will set Lily's mind at ease. Two, I make really great cookies and it might cheer up her friend. It's a small thing and won't take long. What's the worst that can happen? We waste an hour and an elderly person gets a couple dozen cookies as a gift? Besides, you hired me to make her happy, didn't you? Do you want me to drive?"

"Your car doesn't have enough leg room for me." Even his frown couldn't do any damage to Ty's good looks.

"I'll get the cookies." Hannah hurried to the kitchen, glad to get away. She had to admit to herself that she was attracted to Tyler Matthews and it made her very, very nervous. The last thing she needed to leave here with was a broken heart.

* * *

The five-mile ride was filled with awkward silence.

She didn't know what had come over her the past few days. She'd grown more shy around Ty rather than less, no doubt because of the pull she felt toward him. It was more than physical, although that, too, was disconcertingly strong. She found herself wanting to be in his orbit whenever he was home, feeling glad when he spent time with her and Lily, wishing he didn't work quite so hard so he could be at home more often.

She liked to talk with him. He was quick, smart, clever and had a droll sense of humor. He surprised her with his knowledge about so many things, his understanding of the world of business and, particularly, with his compassion. She'd never met a man with such a capacity to love. It all centered around his grandmother, of course, but she could see that he had enough to share with a wife, a family and oh-so-many more and yet never be depleted. It seemed odd that he had chosen not to have that in his life.

All their conversations centered on Lily, which was as it should be, but it unnerved her when she felt him studying her with those piercing blue eyes. She felt revealed under his gaze, as if, when he knew her better he'd be able to read her soul.

Once they'd spent some time together, she hoped she'd learn the thoughts behind those compelling eyes. Perhaps when he became less mysterious to her, she would feel less drawn to him, she consoled herself.

Hannah asked the first question that popped into her head. "What was Lily's marriage to your grandfather like?"

It took him a moment to answer. "Like living inside a valentine."

"How is that?"

"Roses, chocolates, frills and ruffles, kissing, hugging, simpering smiles. All that stuff that horrifies a little boy. I had a lot to get used to."

"Really? They actually behaved that way?"

"Theirs was a true love story. My grandfather ruined Lily for any other man, of course. No one else would have the energy to keep it up. Besides, she was never interested in anyone else."

She and Steve had had their own true love story, Hannah knew. She understood Lily's unwillingness to attempt to replace a love like that.

"The standard they set is high."

"But you've attempted to step into your grandfather's shoes where Lily's care and happiness are concerned."

He shifted in his seat and rolled his shoulders back, as if to make himself more comfortable. "I was young when my grandfather died," he said obliquely.

"What does that mean?"

"I hadn't had much experience with deathbed requests at that time."

She stared at him. He stared straight ahead at the road, his profile somber and chiseled. "I don't understand."

"My grandfather died at home. He asked me to come to his room only hours before he died. I was pretty broken up at the time, naturally. When he asked me to take care of Grams, what else could I say but yes? Then he added, 'Keep her happy, Tyler. It's going to be hard on her when I'm gone. Do all you can, will you?' Of course I agreed."

"And you've been doing so ever since?" Her respect for him went up another notch. It was something she, too, would have done, had she had the chance, even though the cost could be high.

"I would have anyway. My grandparents

were very good to me. But in my mind, I hear my grandfather's voice. That's what keeps me going when Grams is being particularly challenging. I loved him very much. What was important to him is important to me."

"Do you do it because you are a Christian or because your grandfather told you to do it?" Hannah asked curiously.

"Both. God and Gramps have both given me instruction. Who am I to mess with that?"

They were both quiet as they pulled up in front of the house at the address Lily had given them.

"Here we are." It was a simple white house with red shutters and a lawn badly in need of attention.

Hannah was surprised by the simplicity of this home compared with the Matthews house. She supposed she'd assumed all of Lily's friends would have been from the same social class. Hannah was pleased that Lily and Ty didn't seem to find that important.

"Let's get this done," Ty muttered. "I'm not good at being a busybody."

"Only for Lily, right."

"*Only* Lily."

Chapter Nine

Hannah took the big box of cookies she'd packed out of the backseat of the car. "Think of this as bringing a little sunshine into someone's life," she said to Ty.

"Look after widows and orphans in their distress?" He quoted James.

"Exactly." She pressed the doorbell and heard a grating, unmusical sound coming from the back of the house. The door was thrown open and a thirtysomething man with uncombed hair and a scruffy beard appeared.

"We've come to visit Clara," Hannah said. "We have a gift for her from her friend Lily Matthews."

"Let them in, John." An elderly woman in a walker was slowly making her way to the front of the house. Her hair was pulled back in a bun from which flyaway gray hairs had escaped. She'd been pretty once, but time and pain had etched deep creases in her cheeks and around her mouth.

Inside, the place felt grubby. The windows hadn't been washed in some time and were a filmy, cloudy gray.

"Are you Clara?" Hannah asked.

"No. I'm Margaret. Clara is my sister."

Ty stepped forward. "I'm Tyler Matthews. My grandmother Lily and your sister are friends. We have got some baked goods for her."

"She's in her room." The woman pointed toward a hallway. "First door on the left."

Clara was in a rocking chair by the window. Hannah went immediately to the chair and knelt down. "Lily Matthews thought some cookies might cheer you up. I'm Hannah, her caregiver, and this is Ty, Lily's grandson."

Ty reached out a hand to the older woman. "Clara and I have met, but it's been a long time."

"So nice to see you again. This is lovely of her! I did need a pick-me-up today," the white-haired, sweet-faced woman said. "Please sit down and visit a minute—if you can find a place, that is."

Every space was covered with clutter.

"I'm not able to pick up around here, so it's a bit of a mess. My sister said her son, John, should help me, but I'd rather not ask him. It makes him crabby."

"Who is here to care for you and your sister?" Hannah inquired, keeping her tone easy and pleasant.

"No one, except John. Margaret does a little cooking. John's supposed to do the rest. It's to be in lieu of rent because he's living here while he's looking for work."

"Then a little homemade baking will taste good," Hannah said brightly. "Let us tell you about Lily."

They chatted for a bit. Then when they got up to leave, Clara had tears in her eyes. "Thank you so much. You don't know how much your visit has meant to me. Tell Lily thank you."

"Maybe you can come over for a visit one day," Ty suggested. "Lily would love that."

When they got back into the car, Ty was somber. "That poor woman is living a life that's the antithesis of my grandmother's.

And I've been thinking I had it tough keeping up with Lily!"

"Clara's not complaining. Perhaps she has no money or resources to go elsewhere. Maybe she doesn't want to rock the boat."

Lily, however, could wield both her tongue and that cane of hers with the precision and elegance of a rapier. Someone would have received a tongue-lashing a long time ago if those two had changed places.

"In this life, the hardest part is saved for last—aging, illness, failing mind and body," Hannah said softly.

"My grandfather said something almost exactly like that about himself once. Age has a way of diminishing a person, stripping one of strength and vitality. He'd become an old man, looked and acted nothing like the man who had built businesses, fought in wars, done heroic deeds and been a sterling husband and father. Funny, but I hadn't thought about it quite this way before—not, at least, until after Lily broke her foot."

Impulsively, he turned to her. "I'm hungry. Maybe we should get something to eat." He surprised himself at the words coming out of his mouth. He knew all about keeping a professional distance between employer and employee. Yet he'd just asked Hannah to lunch. He assured himself it wasn't a date or anything, just practical. He was hungry. She was probably hungry, too.

"Thank you. That would be very nice."

He drove toward a place that he hadn't been to in years.

"What is this?" Hannah asked as they drove through a parklike setting toward a large white farmhouse with several outbuildings scattered around it.

"A place from my childhood. I haven't been here in years, so I can't promise you the food is good, but the atmosphere is pleasant."

On one side of the road was a miniature golf course, and on the other was a pasture containing miniature goats.

"This is The Farmhouse."

"It certainly is." Hannah stared at the big four-square house with its double-hung windows and green shutters.

"No, I mean, that's its name. The Farmhouse. When I was a kid we'd come here because the food is just like home-cooking. Then my grandmother would go to the gift shop—" he pointed to a building that looked suspiciously like a fancy chicken coop "—while my grandfather and I played miniature golf. We could only play one game, however. Grandfather said that he couldn't afford to let Lily spend any more time in a retail establishment. She usual had a half-dozen packages with her by the time we left as it was."

"What a wonderful memory."

"I guess we'll find out if it's still the same or if it's changed like everything else."

He was tired of changes, he realized, hoping against hope that this one place had stood against the storm of progress.

Chapter Ten

I will have to bring Danny here, Hannah thought as they walked up the stone path to the front door. Children were playing and laughing on an old-fashioned swing set that sat in the side yard. Others were engaged with the small petting zoo run by two pretty teenage girls. Families were eating on a stone patio. She tried to imagine Ty as a small boy, accompanied by a much younger Lily and her husband.

An older woman in a prairie dress and bonnet greeted them at the door. "Two for lunch?"

"Yes, please."

The woman looked at Ty and her eyes narrowed. "Are you Lily Matthew's grandson?"

Ty appeared startled. "Yes, I am. How did you know?"

"I've been greeting people at this door for forty years. You were a beautiful child and now you're a handsome man. Besides, you look just like your grandfather." She thrust out her hand. "I'm Winnie Carlyle. My husband and I own The Farmhouse."

"I'm surprised you recognized me," Ty said as they shook hands.

After he'd introduced Hannah, Winnie said, "You were here almost once a week when you were a child. It would be hard not to see the resemblance." A faraway look flickered in her gaze. "Your grandparents told me that you loved to come here, so they made a point of coming every week. I thought that was very sweet. Of course, the sun rose and set on you, according to them. I don't know if I've ever seen a better-loved child. How are your grandparents now?"

Hannah could see that Ty was touched by that comment. It also gave her a peek into one of the reasons for Ty's devotion to Lily now.

"My grandfather has passed away, but Lily is as much a fireball as ever."

"Oo-weee, we loved to see that woman come into the gift shop, if you know what I mean."

"Perfectly." Ty smiled.

"Say hello to her for me, will you? She was such a gracious lady. It would be fun to see her again."

"Maybe we could come for lunch sometime?" Hannah addressed Ty. "She'd love that."

They ate fried chicken with mashed potatoes and gravy, fresh green beans with almonds, coleslaw, baked beans and strawberry shortcake. Winnie must have given orders to their server because the helpings were huge, their coffee cups stayed full and at the end of the meal, she came out of the kitchen with cake and berries to take to Lily.

Hannah leaned back in her chair, feeling too full to move. "I envy you your history, your background with your grandparents."

His blue eyes widened. "Surely you have good memories of your childhood, too."

"Yes, I had very loving parents. I suppose it's what happened after I grew up that makes me forget those good times."

"I don't understand."

She drew a deep breath. She'd chosen to tell as few people as possible about her and Trisha's past. It was just too painful, even now. But Ty seemed genuinely interested.

"My parents died when I was in college

and I raised Trisha. I was the one trying to make memories for her, but we didn't have a lot of money to go places. There was some insurance money, of course, but I paid for my schooling and our living out of that and it ran out when Trisha was in high school. Fortunately, until recently, I've always had a good job."

"I'm sorry you had to go through that," Ty said sympathetically. His compassionate expression encouraged her to continue.

"My parents had gone on a skiing trip with some friends and rented a chalet. The night before they were to come home, something went terribly wrong in the heating system. In the morning, they didn't wake up, all poisoned by carbon monoxide. I'm ten years older than Trisha, so I was staying with her, babysitting." She felt herself drifting back toward those horrific days. "It was in the news for some time. When all the confusion with the press and the curiosity-seeking died down, I decided that I wasn't going to talk about it anymore. I didn't want that to be the thing that defined either me or my sister. I don't crave pity or sympathy. My parents were Christians. I know where they are and that I'll see them again someday. It was necessary to move on—for Trisha's sake, if not my own."

"So you were mother, father and sister to her?"

"I tried. I don't think I did a very good job sometimes."

"Don't be too hard on yourself. That's a big responsibility for someone so young."

"I know I did some things right. Trisha is a well-rounded, talented girl who has a strong faith."

"Isn't that enough?" He leaned forward, looking at her intently.

"I did a very bad job of instilling common sense in my sister. She's impulsive sometimes and she has very little grasp of finances. I held on to the reins of all that for far too long. In fact, when I moved over to your house, that was the first time I gave Trisha the responsibility of paying the mortgage and utilities."

"Sounds like she's a smart girl, so she'll figure that out."

"It's still an area in which I feel I failed her. It was simply too hard for me to think of everything."

"What about other family members? Couldn't they help you?"

"My parents were both only children. It

was up to me to take care of my sister. Steve was good with her, of course." Hannah pulled herself away from the memories. "At least I'm getting another chance with Danny. That boy will be prepared for anything by the time I'm through raising him." She pushed away from the table. "I think I'd better walk or I'm going to settle here and not be able to get up."

He paid the check and hurried to pull back her chair.

It felt good to be treated this way, Hannah realized, but she'd better not get used to it. Today was an unusual one and likely wouldn't repeat itself.

She groaned as she stepped into the sunlight. "How am I ever going to stay awake this afternoon after eating that huge meal?"

"Maybe we should work it off?" Ty's eyes were twinkling. "I challenge you to a game of miniature golf."

"I thought you were the one who had so much work to do," she teased, delighted that he'd asked. "I'm supposed to be taking over some of your duties, not causing you to have more of them."

"This is for old time's sake. Lily will think it's a hoot when we tell her."

His eyes sparkled, making him downright irresistible. "Well, if it's for Lily…"

Ty took that as a yes, paid three dollars each for the clubs and ushered Hannah onto the course. The first hole was the open mouth of a dinosaur, its head resting on the ground.

"I haven't done this since—" Hannah felt emotion tightening in her throat "—since I did it with my parents when I was a little girl."

Ty took off his suit coat, folded it carefully and handed it to the attendant. Then he began to roll up the sleeves of his finely ironed white shirt. His forearms were muscular and tanned. For the first time Hannah noticed his hands, strong and well-groomed. This man didn't seem to have any flaws whatsoever—except for his impatience and that touchy issue concerning the dent in his Mercedes.

"Do you know how to do this?"

Before she could answer he came around behind her, tucked a club into her left hand and drew her right into position, for all practical purposes, holding her in his arms.

He was wearing that cologne again. The one that Hannah come to associate with him. The one that made her feel a little giddy.

"You first." He gestured toward the box. "Start here."

She weighed the club, obviously made for a child, in her hands and eyed the Tyrannosaur on green number one. The dinosaur was wearing lipstick.

Ty stepped back, but her senses were still rattled.

It wasn't until the third hole that Hannah finally relaxed. By the fourth hole, her competitive spirit had been stoked. She squealed when she timed her ball to go between the blades of a five-foot-high windmill and drop into the cup.

"Yes! I'm winning!"

"Don't get puffed up quite yet, missy," Ty cautioned. He was one hole ahead of her, which displayed a sand trap with a thirsty camel and a wooden palm tree. He eyed the hole at the base of the tree and chipped over the sand.

Hannah watched the ball drop beneath the palm tree and into the hole. "No fair! You've been practicing." Her small chin came out indignantly.

He threw his head back and laughed. "Only for business and on a regular course. I usually get out once or twice a month. Before Lily got hurt, I played every week."

"I need a handicap," she muttered. By the ninth hole, Hannah had completely forgotten that Tyler was her employer. She threw herself into the game with such abandon that nothing mattered but the score.

"Do you want to go another round?" Ty asked as he sunk his ball into the final cup. Then he glanced at his watch and whistled between his teeth. "Or maybe not. I lost track of time."

They were both laughing out loud as they returned to Ty's car. "That's the most fun I've had in ages," Hannah blurted. "I don't know why I didn't think to bring Danny to one of these before. I guess I've been too serious for too long. We'll come back. Danny will like it here as much as you did as a boy."

"Let me know when. Maybe I'll join you." Then they were at his car.

As Hannah slid into the passenger seat, her mind whirred. What did he mean, he'd join them? Why would he want to do that? Granted, Danny was a fun little boy, but Ty himself had admitted he was swamped with work. Perhaps it was because of his own fond memories? That had to be it. Hannah couldn't think of another good reason he'd want to come with them to The Farmhouse.

Now where had that offer come from, Ty wondered as he started the engine. He didn't have two extra minutes in the upcoming days, but he'd offered to go miniature golfing? He must be more exhausted than he'd thought. His mouth was working completely without his brain. Or, a niggling voice said in his head, maybe it *was* his brain working. Hannah St. James was good for his soul.

Lily was, as he'd expected, waiting for them.

"How is she? How's Clara?"

He and Hannah glanced at each other. He would have liked to hide Clara's troubles from Lily, but the truth won out.

"She's got a small, crowded room at the back of the house, which faces north. I don't think a sunbeam could get in there even if it wanted to."

Lily's bright expression faded. "Oh, my."

"Her sister's son, John, is supposed to be taking care of things and driving them places in trade for room and board."

"John? I've heard about him as a teenager.

Clara told me that he was a big loser. She said her sister had a terrible time with him. He was always being picked up for petty theft or starting a fight or vandalism. And *he's* the one taking care of Clara?"

"She says they have pizza or deep fried chicken almost every night, something he picks up at the store."

"Pizza? Clara hates pizza!"

"She loved the cookies, though, Gram. Hannah will bake some more for her."

"I can do nutritious trail mix and things with oatmeal and raisins. Maybe I'll get some meal supplements for her, too. John doesn't need to know."

"I don't think he'd care, even if he did," Ty said dryly.

"My poor, dear friend," Lily moaned. Energy seemed to bleed out of her. Suddenly, she looked all of her ninety years. "I think I'd like to rest now, if you don't mind." She dismissed them with a wave of her hand.

Outside the door Ty muttered, "I've never seen her like that before."

"She's upset. We'll try to lift her spirits after she's had some time alone. She and Danny are friends. He'll cheer her up if I can't."

"Call me if you need me," Ty ordered.

"We won't need you. Just catch up on your work."

He nodded absently, still frowning, and disappeared down the stairs.

Hannah remained in the hallway. What a puzzling, frustrating and delightful day it already had been. Their time at The Farmhouse had been a wonderful respite and Ty's friendly, practically affectionate, behavior had warmed her soul.

What would happen next in this day full of surprises?

Chapter Eleven

Hannah was relieved to hear the front door open on Monday afternoon. Danny was home. She'd done all she could to cheer Lily today, but it hadn't worked very well. Maybe her son could do better. Lily always perked up when Danny was around. No matter what conversation Hannah had started, it always rolled around to Lily's concern for Clara.

"Hey, Mom. What is there to eat?" He dumped his backpack on the kitchen table and opened the refrigerator door. It hadn't taken him long to feel perfectly at home here in this big house. Better yet, he was smiling. That meant no bullies had been after him today. Small for his age, Danny seemed to have more than his share of trouble with bigger, meaner kids.

"Oatmeal raisin cookies, trail mix, cereal bars and morning glory muffins."

"All that? Cool."

"I'm baking for a friend of Lily's. Don't eat everything." She put food on a plate while Danny poured himself a glass of milk. "How was school?"

"Boring. What's Lily doing?"

He asked that every day, Hannah thought with amusement. Lily apparently had a way of charming little boys.

"She's feeling a little sad. A friend of hers isn't doing well. I was hoping you'd have something exciting to tell her about school today."

"Well, the rabbit in the sixth grade room had babies today. That was exciting."

"I should say."

"Especially since they'd named the bunnies Bert and Ernie. My teacher said that one of the bunnies was actually Ernestine."

He said this so innocently that Hannah held back a smile. "Lily would love to hear about that."

Danny grabbed a handful of trail mix. "I'll go tell her. Besides, she told me that she had a plan for us, me and her."

"To do what?"

"I don't know. She acted like it was a big secret. She said I couldn't tell you."

"But you just did."

"No, I didn't. I don't know what she's talking about. Maybe it's a birthday present for you or something."

"I don't think Lily knows when my birthday is, honey. Now go upstairs and tell Lily about Bert and Ernestine."

He obliged happily, and Hannah sent up a word of thanks for her small son. Danny had turned out to be a special gift in this house, her secret weapon when Lily was cross. Then her thoughts turned to Trisha.

Sometimes her sister didn't act her age, she mused grimly. She certainly hadn't been good about keeping in touch. Granted, Hannah hadn't been away long, but Trisha hadn't made any effort to call her. It was always Emma or Jane who answered the house phone when she called. What was Trisha doing with all her time?

She picked up the phone and dialed her home number. Emma answered.

"Hi, Emma, how are things?"

"Good! We love living here."

"Have you had time to look for apartments?"

"We've looked at a few. There are a couple

we like. Of course, we'll need to know when you're coming back before we rent one."

"I'll let you know as soon as I do. If you girls have to stay a couple extra weeks, that's okay, too."

"You're a doll, Hannah."

"Is Trisha around? I'd like to talk to her."

"No, I think she's going to be late. She was on her way to the library. She planned to eat dinner out and then study at Jason's for a while."

"Jason? Who is Jason?"

"He's a good friend of Jane's. She introduced them. He's a nice guy, I think."

"Could this have anything to do with why Trisha is impossible to catch at home?"

"Have you tried her cell?"

"It goes directly to voice mail."

"She hasn't been good about picking up for us either. I know she's been working a lot. Should I tell her to call you when she gets home?"

"Yes, please. It doesn't matter if it's late." Now she felt some urgency about talking to her sister. Trisha had never had a real boyfriend. Surely she wouldn't fall in love now. She needed to finish school first. Then Hannah shrugged it off. She was being overprotective again. Her sister was a big girl. She'd spent so much time and money putting Trisha through school that she probably cared about it as much or more than her sibling. She just hoped this fellow wouldn't distract her already unfocused sister even more.

Here was an area where she and Tyler were alike. He hovered over Lily like she fussed about Trisha. Quite a pair, they were. They both needed to relax.

Danny was still with Lily when Hannah started supper. Hannah had made a pan of enchiladas and was preparing Spanish rice when Ty walked into the kitchen.

"Home already? I thought you were working." Her mind flashed back to a time when Steve would walk into her kitchen and she would say those very words to him. Of course, he'd also taken her in his arms and kissed her soundly. Ty's arms around her at the miniature golf course came to mind. She'd felt surprisingly safe and warm there, too.

"I told my secretary to tell everyone I was out for the afternoon. I got much more work done than I'd expected. Besides, I wondered if Lily was still worrying about her friend."

"She was until Danny came home. Now they're cloistered up there and won't let me in. I heard giggling through the door, but they chased me away. Danny said Lily told him she had something planned, something secret."

"Uh-oh. I don't like the sound of that."

"What kind of trouble can a little boy and an old woman get into?"

"Plenty. I grew up with her, remember? We used to drive Gramps crazy with Gram's schemes."

"She's older now and doesn't have so much energy," Hannah assured him.

He looked at her with a doubtful smile and grazed her cheekbone with the back of his finger. "I think you're underestimating her, but you'll find out for yourself sooner or later."

"Fine. I will. Now why don't you go upstairs and bring our troublemakers down for dinner?"

It was nice to come home to the aromas of dinner cooking and the sound of someone moving around the kitchen, Tyler thought, as he headed up the stairs. Irene usually left something in the refrigerator to heat up, but that wasn't quite the same. In her day, Lily had been quite a cook, but she'd grown less and less interested as she'd aged. Seeing Hannah there, wrapped in one of Lily's old aprons, made him nostalgic. And Hannah smelled even better than the delicious aromas in the room—lilacs? Or was it lavender again?

Shaking off the wistfulness, Tyler knocked on the bedroom door.

"Who is it?" Lily called, sounding suspicious.

"Who do you think it is?"

"Oh, Tyler, it's you. You're home early."

It used to be that he could never get home early enough for his grandmother. Now he wasn't so sure.

"Hannah says dinner is ready. Do you want to come downstairs or have me bring a tray upstairs?"

He could hear whispered muttering and then the door flew open. Danny was on the other side, standing like a gatekeeper between Ty and his grandmother.

"I'll take a tray in my room. I'm very tired tonight. Danny, go tell your mother."

The child nodded sharply, although Ty had a hunch he'd considered saluting. Whatever these two were hatching was going to be played out with military precision. Heaven help us, Tyler thought.

"Feeling better, Grandmother?"

"Good as can be expected, considering the circumstances. I'm just sick about Clara, but Danny is good medicine."

"He told Hannah you had something planned. You aren't going to get him into trouble, are you?"

Her eyes narrowed and a crafty look spread across her features. "Never you mind, Tyler."

"You got me in trouble more than once when I was a kid."

"I was younger then, silly. Now I'm wise and mature." She gave a throaty sound. "Too mature, I think."

She sat silently for a moment before she spoke again. "We have to help my friend, Ty. I'm practically helpless right now, so you will have to be the one to do it."

He sighed and leaned over to kiss her cheek. "I'll think about it, Gram, but I don't know what I can do."

"Hannah is smart. She can help you."

"I hired her to take care of *you*."

"That will be taking care of me, Ty. Helping Clara will be good for my heart."

He met Hannah on the stairs. She was carrying a tray with Lily's food, flatware, a pot of tea and a single flower.

"Careful. You're setting a new standard. She won't get flowers after you leave, I'm afraid."

She smiled at him. "Then I'll train Irene to do it. Women love flowers. You'd be remiss if you didn't bring her a flower on her tray."

He looked amused. "What's your favorite flower, Hannah?"

She was about to say roses because Steve had always brought her roses. He'd called them "our flower." But she wanted to hold that information close to her heart. Sometimes she couldn't even quite remember Steve's features that she'd once so loved.

"Irises, daffodils, orchids, daisies, geraniums and pansies." That should cover all the bases.

"That would make quite a bouquet."

She smiled shyly and changed the subject. "I'll be right down to dish up for the rest of us."

As he went toward the kitchen, Ty marveled at how quickly he'd become accustomed to her and Danny living here. It was cozy, welcoming and full of life with her here. Ty could easily get used to this.

Danny was particularly chatty at the table. He said the table prayer and then just kept talking. He told Ty about Bert and Ernestine, about a scuffle on the playground and about the girls who'd been bugging him lately. Hannah was silent.

When she sent Danny upstairs to take a shower before bed, Ty stayed at the table. "More coffee or dessert?" she asked.

"Sure. And a little conversation about Lily and Clara." She nodded and he noticed her relax. Sometimes Hannah reminded him of a deer—beautiful, skittish and shy. Until she felt secure, then, look out.

"I want to go back. I've prepared food for her."

"Should I come along?" He could hear Lily's mandate ringing in his ears.

"If John is there, you might be able to distract him so I could talk to Clara privately. Lily has some questions she wants me to ask her."

They stayed at the table, not speaking, for some time. It was a contented silence,

Ty noted. He hadn't experienced a comfortable silence with a woman for a long time, he thought with some irony. And when he found it, it was with his employee, his grandmother's nurse.

Chapter Twelve

At midnight Hannah dialed Trisha's cell phone number again. It was still off. She'd been trying all day, and she was getting angry. She'd left messages with Emma and Jane on the home phone and several on Trisha's cell in the past week and a half and she'd never called back. This newfound freedom had apparently gone to Trisha's head. She knew Trisha was healthy and attending school—her roommates had assured Hannah of that. Still, she considered it the ultimate in rudeness to not acknowledge a call or message, and Trisha knew it. She'd been at the Matthews home for nearly a month and had only talked to her sister a couple times.

She turned off her own phone and the bedside lamp and settled into the downy softness of her pillows. She had a bad feeling about this, but she wasn't sure why. She also had concerns about the relationship between her and her new boss.

They were being thrown together so much that it was difficult to keep a professional distance, especially when she felt about him as she did. And how was that? She refused to actually consider what might sum it up best. Attraction. Infatuation. It would be easy to fall in love with a man like Ty.

She slept restlessly and woke up early feeling like she hadn't shut her eyes all night. Hannah stumbled, head down, into the kitchen in her sweats and bare feet looking for coffee and ran face-first into Ty. His shirt smelled of soap, starch and shaving lotion. That woke her up faster than a double shot of espresso. She turned quickly, avoiding his eyes, as if her thoughts of last night were somehow written there.

"Sorry. I wasn't watching where I was going. I was just following my nose to the coffee." She felt herself blush.

"I peeked in on my grandmother. She's not up yet."

"I'll go up after my run." She scraped her fingers through her hair, a little embarrassed to be caught in her oldest sweats, with her hair looking as if it had been stirred with a hand mixer.

"I carved out some time today to go on those trivial errands Lily's been thinking up. We can also stop at Clara's."

Lily had been peculiar lately, asking the two of them to run strange errands—like asking Hannah to pick up fresh fruit from the garden center and, oh, yes, please take Ty with her, so he could bring home a few sacks of potting soil while they were at it. Or insisting she needed a certain book that only Hannah could pick out at the warehouse store—and insisting Ty accompany her to bring home a fifty-pound bag of rice.

Danny had been odd, too. He'd begun setting the dinner table with place cards, making sure that Hannah and Ty always sat next to each other at the table.

Of course, Hannah thought that she'd been no prize either lately, worrying about Trisha. What had happened to her reliance on that verse in Matthew? *Therefore I tell you, do not worry about your life.*

God was handling it. She was just uneasy because *she* didn't know what He was going to do next.

"How about I pick you up at three?" Ty said before he left for work. "Sorry I have to go in early today." They'd begun having coffee after their run, something that Hannah looked forward to every day. "Irene will stay with Lily and Danny while we pick up Lily's weird list. I wonder what she's up to."

Lily was throwing them together at every opportunity, Hannah thought. Danny, too, come to think of it.

"I called Trisha earlier and made her promise to be at the house at four-thirty. I need to talk to that girl." Though she'd never told him the whole scoop, Ty had probably put two and two together by now—that she was deeply concerned about her sister's behavior.

"Then we'll stop there, too. I have got some traveling coming up. We might as well get everything done now while we can."

"Will you be gone long?"

"A couple days, probably."

She would miss him, she realized. Their relationship had become important to her.

At a little after three, she found herself in the local discount warehouse store tagging after Ty.

"What does Lily want with fifty pounds of rice and huge bags of potting soil?" Ty asked.

"I could have taken care of everything on this list, except for those heavy things." Hannah appeared rueful. "I'm sorry to bother you with this."

"That's probably what she wanted—a reason for us to go shopping together. She's brewing something up." Ty sounded resigned. "As long as we're out, do you mind if I stop at the men's store and pick up a couple shirts for my next trip?"

"Sure. Why not?" It would bring back memories. She hadn't been in a men's store since her husband died seven years ago. Steven had been a bit of a clotheshorse and she knew everything that those type of stores exuded—the smells of new fabric and the warm, familiar odor of freshly pressed clothing, the long racks of men's suits, jackets and trousers, the tables of vivid ties and the masculinity.

Maybe it was time to face the memories she'd avoided for so long. She really didn't understand why she'd waited so long to confront these small things. Her head felt clogged with them and they crowded her heart and mind just when she needed both to be open to change, to the future. She was a different woman now, stronger, more independent than she'd been back then. All her troubles hadn't cowed her. They'd nearly knocked her to her knees a few times, but she'd kept getting up.

When they reached the store that afternoon, she raised her chin, thrust it forward and marched in.

Ty, seeming to notice the physical shift in her, reached out and took her arm as if to give her internal strength. Sometimes she wondered if he could read her mind.

"I need a couple of ties, too," Ty said. "Do you mind picking some out for me? Whatever you think is best."

"Me?"

"You have good taste, don't you?"

"Well, yes, but—"

"Then use it to pick out the ties." He gave her an encouraging grin, took her shoulders and turned her until she pointed toward the ties. Then he walked off in another direction.

She knew exactly what he needed. Her hand went immediately to a tie with the vivid blue color of his eyes swirled into the contemporary design. The second tie she chose was a more traditional repeating pattern, but it also had a touch of that remarkable blue. She ran a finger across the fine silk. It felt good. It made her feel like a wife again.

Quashing that thought, she brought them to the counter as Ty was conversing with the salesman.

"How about these?" She laid them out before him.

Ty stared at them silently.

It was the clerk who spoke. "Perfect! Absolutely perfect! I wouldn't have done any better. Your girlfriend has excellent taste."

Girlfriend? She rather liked the sound of it. Rather than correct him, they played along.

As they neared the exit door, Ty put his arm around Hannah's shoulder. "Let me escort you to the door, *girlfriend,*" he said good-humoredly.

As he touched her, she felt something shimmer through her body, a feeling she hadn't experienced in years—attraction, magnetism. Hannah had thought she was long past that powerful yearning, that it had died with Steve. She was flummoxed to realize that it was alive and well and radiating between her and Ty.

"One more stop," Hannah said. "If Trisha isn't home, I plan to track her down if it takes all night."

"You didn't mention that when we started out," he said mildly.

"If she's not there, I'll have you take me home to get my car," she assured him. "I'm just not going to let her avoid me any longer."

As they pulled up to the front of Hannah's house Jane walked outside. When she saw them, her face registered an odd expression.

"She doesn't look very happy to see us," Ty commented.

"Too bad. I've decided those girls are helping Trisha hide something. I'm having no pity on any of them today." She waved Jane over before she had time to duck into the house and warn Trisha.

"Hi, Hannah. We weren't expecting you," Jane said uneasily.

"No? Good. My sister has been avoiding me. It's time for me to find out why."

"It's not like that."

Hannah cut her off. "Where is she?"

"In her room, sleeping."

"At this time of day? She'll be up all night."

Jane didn't say anything.

Ty trailed the two women into the house. They found Trisha coming down the stairs, tousled with bed head, her eyes puffy and wrinkled sheet marks embedded in the side of her face. She'd been sleeping hard.

It didn't seem to have done her much good, Hannah thought. Her sister looked dreadful. The bags under her eyes had bags. She'd lost weight and her color was slightly ashen. She didn't *look* like she'd been having a good time partying since Hannah had left the house.

"Honey, are you okay? Have you been sick? Is that why you haven't called?"

Trisha flushed. "No. I guess I've just been busy."

The sisters stared at each other, their expressions both challenging and unhappy.

"It's nice out today. I think I'll just take this magazine and wait outside on the front porch," Ty said calmly, "and let you two visit."

Hannah nodded and watched him escape before turning to her sister. "Okay, what's going on?"

"Who says anything is going on?" Trisha retorted truculently.

"I do. You're avoiding me. You aren't home early in the morning or late at night. Jane and Emma seem more and more vague about you every time I call. Either you have them lying for you or they don't know what's going on either. I'm not leaving here until I get an explanation for your behavior."

"I've been studying, okay? I'm getting straight As so far."

"Good for you. For the money and effort we've put into this, you should be." Hannah rarely showed her temper, but Trisha had pushed her far enough. "But I doubt that even you could study *that* much. Where have you been? What's going on? And who is Jason?"

To Hannah's surprise, Trisha's expression seemed to melt from defensiveness to something closer to fear. What was going on in her little sis's life?

"I got a job. Okay? Is that so bad?"

"A job doing what? I thought we'd decided that with your full load, you shouldn't take on any more than your small part-time waitress work to be sure to keep your grades up?"

"A couple things, no big deal."

"It is to me. Don't lie to me, Trisha. I've been worried about you. I can never get you on the phone and you never call me."

"I'm cleaning offices, that's all. I can't do them until after ten at night, so I just stay at the library until then and go to work before I come home. And you know that we have to turn off our cell phones in the library."

"There is such a setting as vibrate," Hannah said dryly. "And why on Earth did you take on a job? You know we agreed that…"

"Not a job, jobs," Trisha corrected softly. "I have two jobs."

Now Hannah was truly dumbfounded.

"I also work at another coffee shop near the campus. I'm the one who opens at 5:00 a.m. I'm done before classes start, so it works out perfectly."

"You call it working out perfectly when you work at one job until midnight, start another at 5:00 a.m., go to school all day and study all evening? That sounds more like torture to me! What are you thinking? And why didn't you tell me?"

"I thought I could work it out, that's all. I didn't want you to know." Tears brimmed in Trisha's eyes and her lips quivered. She suddenly looked like she was ten years old.

Hannah softened. "Work out what, honey? What's wrong?"

To Hannah's surprise, her sister dissolved into a flood of tears and weeping. Her shoulders shook, her body trembled and the sobs sounded as if they were coming from the very core of her. Hannah hurried to put her arms around the girl and held her tightly. When the crying waned, Hannah managed to lift her sister's face to hers and look into her eyes. "Tell me what's wrong."

"I didn't want you to know, Hannah, about how stupid and careless and irresponsible I've been!"

"What did you do?"

"Remember how you told me that I was in charge of the bills for the house now? That I should pay the mortgage, the water, electricity and all that?"

"Perfectly. I left the bills on my desk."

"I must have let it go in one ear and out the other." Trisha's voice was small. "Because I forgot about it until I got bills for the next month and they all had previous balances. They'd *doubled!*"

Hannah refrained from telling her that that was what bills were wont to do.

"I've spent very little out of my account since I moved to the Matthews," she said calmly, although her heart was racing. "I just deposited another paycheck. The bank statements are coming here—you can check for yourself how much is in there. It should be plenty."

Trisha remained silent too long.

"Trish, you didn't…"

"We just went shopping a couple times, Hannah. Emma and Jane were buying these cool leather purses and I found one, too."

"How much?"

"Three hundred dollars."

Hannah had never owned a bag that cost more than fifty dollars in her entire life. She was stunned.

"And Jason and I started dating a little. He's a nice guy, Hannah. A Christian. We mostly meet at the library to study, but sometimes we decided to take a break and go somewhere to eat. Jason likes Calliope." She named the most trendy and expensive café near campus. "He doesn't have much money, though, so I thought it would be okay if I treated. I just put it on the credit card. I never really looked at what things cost until I got the monthly bill."

"What are you saying, Trish?"

"There isn't enough money left to pay the mortgage, Hannah, not for even one month and especially not for two." Before Hannah could open her mouth, Trisha added, "That's why I took the jobs, Han. They're both part-time and by next month I can have most of one month's mortgage paid off. I'm afraid they'll just have to wait a little longer for the rest."

"Trisha," Hannah said sternly, not even trying to keep the horror and dismay out of her voice. "Banks just don't wait until people get around to paying their mortgages! They will be sending me irate letters before long. Do you realize that what you've done could ruin my credit rating?" Hannah felt a catch in her voice. "After how hard I've worked to keep it up? And I could lose my house!"

"I am so dumb!" Trisha, in tears, flung herself back against the couch. Then she looked up. "Maybe we could get someone to loan us the money?"

"Let's get the numbers together—the bills, the mortgage, what you have earned. I'll put it with that paycheck I just deposited and we'll see where it takes us. Come over to the house tomorrow. Mr. Matthews will be out of town. We'll sit down and figure out where we are."

"I'll return the purse," Trisha said in a small voice, "and the other stuff I haven't opened."

"You bet you will," Hannah said grimly. "I'd have you return all that food from Calliope, too, if I could."

Trisha was weeping and Hannah was still

trembling when she left the house. Tyler was sitting on a rocker reading the magazine he'd picked up.

"Did you get things settled?" he asked. "I learned everything there is to know about the charms of a convection oven, the latest wrinkle treatments and what to do if I ever get hormonal. Don't you have any sports or mechanics magazine around here?" he joked.

Hannah tried to gather her wits. It only alarmed her more that what she really wanted to do was fall into his arms and sob.

Chapter Thirteen

"Are you okay? You look terrible," Ty said when they got into the car.

"Thanks a bunch—that makes me feel much better."

"Well, you do."

"Other than being furious with my sister, I'm just fine."

"Want to talk about it?"

"You don't need to be bothered with her antics. Suffice it to say, she's much more immature than I gave her credit for being. I'm a failure as a parent!"

"I don't think it's you who has failed. At some point kids have to take responsibility for their own actions. She's in college. It's time."

"I always tried to protect her from things. Apparently, I protected her too much."

Ty looked at her expectantly, but she didn't continue. They rode in silence to Clara's place. It was suspicious, Ty mused, that it was these little errands for Lily and Clara that consistently threw he and Hannah together. Still, he was beginning to look forward to Lily's to-do lists.

It took John a long time to come to the door. He opened it a crack and mumbled his usual greeting, "Whatdayawant?"

"How's Clara today?"

"What do you want to know for?" He was even more surly than usual. "She's sleeping."

"My grandmother sent her another gift," Ty said with exaggerated patience.

"Clara hasn't used the last gift she sent."

Hannah could see by the set of John's shoulders and his mulish expression that today wasn't the day to argue. She pulled on Ty's sleeve. "Come on, we'll come back another day. When *John* is feeling better."

She thrust a prettily wrapped box into the man's hands. "It's a new blouse. A pink one. Please give it to her."

John scowled, grabbed the box and closed the door in their faces.

"Can't we report him for something?"

"Not unless we have something to report.

Clara hasn't complained. She seems grateful to have a place to live." She pulled on his sleeve again. "Come on. There's nothing more we can do here today."

Ty had already left for the airport when Hannah arose the next morning. She puttered around the kitchen, making coffee, soft-boiled eggs and toast for Lily. When Irene arrived, she carried the breakfast upstairs.

When Irene returned to the kitchen, Hannah was sitting at the table, her hands wrapped around a mug, staring out the patio doors into the garden.

"It's different without him, isn't it?" Irene said, not having to define who she was discussing with Hannah. "The house always feels, oh, *full* when he's here. It's like his personality takes up the extra space. There's more laughter and," Irene smiled, "more *orders* when he's here." Orders that usually contradicted Lily's.

A crafty look lingered on Irene's face. "He likes you. I can see it. He likes you a lot."

"How long have you worked here, Irene?" Hannah asked in an attempt to divert the older woman. That was good to hear, but she didn't want to make too much of it.

"Since Mr. Ty was in college. He's grown into a fine man."

Undeniably.

"What are you and Lily going to do today?" Irene took a small pork roast out of the freezer to thaw.

"I'm not sure. I'll let Lily choose."

"She loves it that you're here, you and that darling boy of yours. It's what she's always dreamed of, you know."

"What do you mean?"

"She's always wanted another woman in this house—and children. A granddaughter-in-law and great-grandchildren."

"We're hardly that."

"It's the closest she's ever come."

Hannah simply couldn't resist. "Why do you think that is?"

"He had someone he'd planned to marry once."

Hannah leaned forward, listening intently.

"Miss Anita was a beautiful woman," Irene recalled. "She could have been a model, that one, but what was best about her was her heart. Pure gold. Ty was head over heels in love. They were young, of course, but I could tell he believed she was The One. He believed that he and Anita could have a marriage like his grandparents had, and that was something he's always wanted.

"Well, Anita and a girlfriend decided that they'd have one last fling before the wedding, so they went to Paris. Anita planned to buy her wedding dress there. It was all very exciting and romantic and then…"

"Go on," Hannah encouraged, rapt.

"They rented a car so they could see the countryside and had a terrible accident. Both were killed."

"How awful!"

"I've never seen a more broken man than Mr. Ty after that. He came to grips with it after many, many months but he has never truly believed there was anyone else for him. Anita was not only his fiancée, but his soul mate. When he couldn't have her, he turned all that intensity and love he'd showered Anita with onto Lily. He didn't want to look for someone new because he didn't believe she existed."

Irene frowned. "If you ask me, he's been hiding behind his responsibility for Lily all these years. He dates but never lets anyone close. He rarely brings someone by to meet his grandmother. I don't think he wants to go through that kind of heartbreak again so he doesn't allow relationships to get too deep.

"By now it's habit, I'm sure. He's just not interested in going through anything like that again."

Hannah understood. She'd experienced much the same thing after Steve's death. Being alone was preferable to being devastated again. She'd trained herself to ignore signals that could draw her to someone else. Hannah had built a tidy, cozy little shell around herself that she never left. Pity the poor man who tried to get by that.

Yet Ty had somehow managed to get by her defenses without her even realizing it. Perhaps it was because he'd had a similar hurt and had built his own shell and knew the barriers that needed to be broken down. He was more like her than she'd ever dreamed.

Hannah considered her response before voicing it. "It's rather sad, isn't it? Having this big, beautiful house with only the two of them in it?"

"Very sad. This house needs babies, not just wheelchairs."

That comment put images in Hannah's head that she didn't want to visit. Ty, babies, someone new for Lily to spoil.

When she went to Lily's room to help her dress, Lily seemed restless.

Hoping to cheer her, Hannah said, "Today is your day. What do you want to do? A movie? Checkers? Knit?"

"I want to visit Clara."

Alarm bells went off in Hannah's head. One of the things that Ty had expressly ordered was that Lily not go out until after her next clinic appointment. It was his overprotective streak, Hannah thought, but he believed Lily was safer at home. That might be good for her physical health, Hannah knew, but not her mental one.

"Your grandson will be back in a few days. Maybe he can take you—"

"Ty is a ball and chain around my neck!" Lily protested. "He treats me like I'm porcelain, not flesh and blood. He learned that from my husband, bless his heart, but I'm sick of being somebody's china doll. *I want to see my friend.*"

"There's no guarantee that John will let us in." She thought about yesterday. "He's not very friendly."

"All the more reason to drop by. What does he have to hide?"

"I don't think it's wise, Lily."

"Well, I do!"

Lord, what have I gotten myself into now? Help!

Irene called from downstairs at that moment, giving Hannah a chance to escape. Lily's chin was set stubbornly and her eyes were narrow. Hannah had no idea how she was going to get out of this one.

It was a miserable day and an even more miserable night. Lily refused to go anywhere or do anything except see Clara.

Lily could be contrary in ways Hannah had never imagined.

Even Irene remarked about it. "She sent back both her breakfast and lunch trays. She hasn't done that in a very long time."

"How long?" Hannah asked wearily. Lily had also refused to bathe and dress or even brush her teeth, at least not unless Hannah agreed that she could visit her friend.

"When Ty's grandfather was alive, she used to do it every once in a while. Of course, the men always give in right away. You're much more determined to outlast her than they were. They knew better. They already knew they couldn't outlast Lily."

"Never?"

"Not that I remember."

"Then I really blundered into it, didn't I?"

"I think so."

"What am I supposed to do, Irene? Ty doesn't want her leaving the house."

"He's a little unreasonable, too, don't you think? I see where he gets it. He's bound to have inherited some of his grandmother's traits."

Only Danny was allowed into Lily's room that evening. At about seven o'clock Hannah managed to have him "sneak" in some snacks for him and Lily—granola bars and ice cream cups, things she was sure Lily would think were Danny's doing and not her own.

After Danny went to bed, Hannah decided it was time to confront this issue head on.

"I didn't invite you in," Lily said sourly when Hannah burst into her room.

"Sorry, but I don't need an invitation. I'm hired to carry out Ty's orders, remember?"

"Then you are both being silly. I'm not a prisoner!"

"Of course not. But I'm not comfortable doing something he expressly forbade."

Lily must have seen the turmoil on her face because she said gently, "I realize that, dear, but Ty doesn't know everything. My heart literally hurts for my friend. I have to see her. It's as much for me as it is for her. Please understand."

Hannah did understand. What's more, she thought Ty was ridiculously overprotective. Of course, Lily was all he had left. Could she blame him?

"You didn't eat today. Can I get you some soup? A sandwich?"

"I don't plan to eat until I see Clara."

"You can't starve yourself." Ty would be livid if that happened.

"I certainly can. You won't force-feed me. He'll only be gone a few days and that will convince him when he comes back that he can't make such rules for me anymore."

What would be worse? Taking Lily to see Clara, or having Ty come home to discover that Lily was on a hunger strike? She shuddered to consider.

Hannah slept little, thinking about what she should do. She prayed for an answer, but none seemed forthcoming. By morning she had a raging headache and no idea what would face her in Lily's room.

Irene was there when Hannah arrived, concern written on her face. "She won't get up, Miss Hannah!"

Lily was firmly planted in her bed, arms crossed, expression daring anyone to obstruct her.

"Lily, you can't…"

"I can and I will. Take me to see Clara and I'll be good as a lamb. Please, Hannah?"

There was a pleading note in the old woman's voice that Hannah couldn't miss. It might be worse not to take her, she realized. Lily was working herself into a tizzy.

"You'll be a lamb? An angel? A perfectly obedient patient?"

"Oh, yes. You know me!"

That was the trouble—Hannah did know Lily. She wasn't sure that Lily was even capable of behaving.

In for a dime, in for a dollar, Hannah thought, as she helped Lily dress for their adventure. She'd gone too far to back out now, even though she was afraid what this might cost her.

Chapter Fourteen

"I'm so happy you finally saw reason, dear," Lily said happily as they drove down the street to Clara's house.

"I didn't see reason. I just had to decide about the lesser of two evils," Hannah said miserably. "You making yourself sick, or Ty yelling at me."

"If my grandson fusses, I'll tell him a thing or two. I know he's being good to me, but it drives me crazy sometimes." She turned to Hannah, her eyes twinkling. "Actually, I'm not nearly the spoiled old lady Ty thinks I am. I'm much more reasonable than he realizes, but he expects it of me so I give him want he wants."

"Lily!"

"Don't tell him, dear, and ruin his fun."

Hannah groaned inwardly. Lily had both of them right where she wanted. And right now, she wanted to be with Clara.

They pulled up to the house and parked.

Clara's sister greeted them at the front door. "Hello, Hannah. Who have we here?"

"This is Clara's friend, Lily. Mr. Matthews's grandmother."

Margaret clapped her hands in delight. "Oh, my goodness! I've heard so much about you! Please come in."

They made their way slowly to Clara's room because of Lily's bad foot—and, Hannah thought—because Lily was taking her time, eyeing the place. It was tidied up as it usually was, but the ever-present grime was still there. It looked as though someone had spilled grease on the hallway carpet recently and it was in dire need of a cleaning.

At the door, Lily turned to Hannah, "I'd like to be alone with her if you don't mind."

"Of course not." Hannah knocked, opened the door and helped Lily to a chair. The cry of delight from Clara assured her that they'd both be all right.

Hannah returned to the living room and Margaret handed her a cup of coffee. "It sounds like my sister was glad to see her friend."

"It seems so." Hannah accepted the cup.

Margaret seemed as hungry for conversation as her sister, but after an hour of chatting, Hannah decided to check on Lily and Clara.

The two women were sitting together, poring over an old photo album, gray heads touching.

"It's probably time to go, Lily," Hannah said gently.

Lily put her hand over Clara's. "I'll be back, don't you worry."

The look they exchanged nearly broke Hannah's heart.

Lily said nothing until they were back in the car. Then she laid her head against the seat and closed her eyes. "It's worse than I thought. She's so lonely and stuck in that tiny room. That lazy nephew does nothing for her. Oh, Hannah, it breaks my heart! We have to do something to help her."

"Did she *ask* for help?"

"No, of course not. She's grateful to have a place to live."

"Then what can you do?"

"I don't know yet, but I will figure it out." There was steely determination in Lily's voice—and something else, something Hannah hadn't heard before. "There are homes, facilities, places where Clara will get better care. I just need to find something suitable."

She looked sharply at the old woman who sounded as though she was short of breath. She was pale and clammy and rubbing her arm as if it hurt her. "Lily, are you okay?"

"Just upset, dear. I'll go home and lay down for a bit and everything will be fine. I didn't mean to become so worked up but... Oh!" Lily pressed her hand to her chest.

"Are you having pain?"

"No, dear, just a little heaviness. I do believe that someone *can* actually have a broken heart."

Hannah made a quick decision. She turned the steering wheel to the right and headed for the emergency room.

"Where are we going?" Lily asked. Her voice wasn't as strong as it had been.

"To see a doctor. I should never have taken you to that house. You've gotten yourself all worked up."

Lily didn't respond. Instead, she settled her head against the backrest and closed her eyes. That frightened Hannah most of all.

It didn't take long, once Hannah told the E.R. receptionist that Lily was having chest pains, for them to find themselves in an examination cubicle with Lily hooked up to an EKG machine.

A doctor entered the cubicle carrying Lily's chart. Both women looked at him expectantly.

"The good news is that Lily seems to be doing fine now. It could have been an anxiety attack she experienced, but I want her to spend the night in the hospital so we can watch her. We'll hook her up to a monitor that will give us an idea what her heart is doing. If things look good, she can go home in the morning."

"That's not necessary!" Lily protested. "I have Hannah if I don't feel well."

"You're staying," Hannah said bluntly. "I feel bad enough for taking you to Clara's. I will not take you out of this hospital before the doctor discharges you."

"It's so much more comfortable at home. And I promised Danny we'd play checkers after school."

The doctor suppressed a smile. "I do think she's going to be fine, but I have to make sure. Twenty-four hours, that's all."

Lily gave him the same look she used with

Hannah and Ty when she didn't agree with one of them.

For once, Lily didn't get her way.

Hannah, who had chosen to remain at the hospital with Lily, tried Ty's cell phone at least once an hour, but he didn't pick up. She didn't want to leave him a message about Lily. She needed to explain things herself. Trisha and one of her roommates had promised to stay with Danny and get him off to school in the morning.

Lily was already sleeping peacefully when Hannah settled herself with a pillow and blanket on the recliner in the room that she'd made into a quasi-bed. She tried to sleep, but all she could think of was that Ty would be furious once he heard that his grandmother had spent the night in the hospital. Her thoughts raced in circles. Lily had been desperate to see her friend. Still, Hannah was the one in change of Lily's health. Even though Lily could talk paint off a wall if she chose to, Hannah knew she had caved in way too soon.

Ty would fire her and she deserved it. Even though it seemed that something special was growing between them, that shouldn't prevent him from firing her. She'd let him down. Lily could die, for goodness' sake! And it would be Hannah's fault. Just when she needed the money to cover Trisha's negligence, Hannah had made the poorest decision of her career. The longer she thought about it, the more convinced Hannah was that *she* was the one for whom a heart attack was imminent.

Lord, You'll have to work this out for me. I put it in Your capable hands. I pray that, whatever happens, it is Your will.

Finally, she slept.

Ty was exhausted. He'd had late meetings and early ones, too much coffee and too little sleep. He was looking forward to getting home and sleeping in his own bed, having breakfast with Danny before he went to school and a relaxing second cup of coffee with Hannah prior to going to the office. They'd fallen into that little routine gradually, and now it seemed almost wrong not to have the ritual to start the day.

It was difficult to go to work with a bad attitude after spending time with Hannah and Danny. They were both excited for every new day and took nothing for granted. Sunshine, rain, fresh muffins, stale cookies, it didn't matter, they were thankful for it all. Being short on money had not made either of them bitter, only grateful.

There was a lesson to be learned there, Ty realized. Of course, there were a lot of lessons he could learn from Hannah. Cheerfulness, patience, transparency, kindness, goodness, persistence, lack of complaint. What's more, her son modeled exuberance, joy and curiosity. Being poor didn't mean having to go without the things that really mattered. He was filled with unexpected warmth and anticipation at the notion of seeing them again. He'd really missed them. His days had felt empty because he couldn't see them.

What was he going to do when Hannah and Danny moved out?

He pulled into the garage and, feeling like a lovesick puppy, grabbed his bag and ran into the house. The kitchen was clean and silent, but the patio door into the backyard was cracked open. His heart beat faster. *Hannah*... Ty put down his things and stepped outside.

Irene and Danny were working together in the late-afternoon sun, picking debris out of the garden. Danny's towhead glinted pale and golden in the sunlight. His earnest, eight-year-old face was expressive, as if he were telling Irene the most important tale in the world.

"Hey, you two!" Ty yelled.

They looked up in unison.

To Ty's surprise, neither of them looked happy to see him. In fact, they appeared downright dismayed.

He walked across the lawn that was Lily's pride and joy. She and the gardener spent hours every summer hatching up new plantings and coming up with ways to foil ash borers and encourage the roses. "What's up?"

Irene and Danny stared at him as if he'd asked them to quote all of Shakespeare's sonnets.

Danny spoke first. "We're cleaning up out here."

"Yes, cleaning," Irene echoed.

"Aren't you here kind of late today, Irene?"

She looked confused and glanced at her watch. "I suppose I am. It's a, er, special occasion."

"What's that?"

"Cleaning the yard," they both said.

"Okay, what are you two up to?" Ty chuckled. "You're acting as if you didn't expect to see me."

"We thought you were coming home *lots later* tonight. You're early," Danny said accusingly.

"I was done and there was space on an earlier flight. Are Lily and Hannah upstairs?" He couldn't hide the excitement in his voice.

Ty saw the pair glance at each other as if they were wondering how to answer.

"They aren't home yet."

"Not at home? Where did they go?"

Before either of them could answer, they heard the honk of a horn out front.

"That's Mom!" Danny chirruped and bolted off.

Ty and Irene followed at a slower pace.

Why, Ty wondered, was Irene wringing her hands?

Chapter Fifteen

Hannah's heart sank when she saw Ty exit the house. She'd hoped to have Lily home and back in her room before Ty arrived. Oh, well, it was what it was. And it was too late now.

"Hey," Ty greeted them cheerfully. He went to Lily's door and opened it. Then he gave his grandmother a peck on the cheek and lifted her out of the car as if she were a toy. "Do you want to go to your room or be downstairs?"

"My room, please," Lily said faintly, her voice tired.

He looked at her curiously but said no more.

Hannah exchanged a frantic look with Irene as they entered the house. This was not working out. Lily was exhausted. If she'd already been asleep when Ty arrived, it would have been much better. That would have given them a few extra hours for Lily to revive.

When she got to the room, Lily was waving Ty off. "Let Hannah help me get ready for bed, dear. I'm very tired."

He looked confused but obediently backed toward the door. "I'll be back in a few minutes."

"Maybe you don't have to tell him what happened," Lily suggested when she and Hannah were alone.

"Of course I do."

"Then tell him it was all my idea."

"I'm touched that you want to protect me, Lily, but I'm responsible for my actions. I shouldn't have taken you to Clara's yesterday. You got too overwrought, and look what happened."

"I don't want my grandson to be upset with you," Lily fretted.

"Let me take care of that," Hannah told her. "I'll tuck you in and then I'll go and face the music." Gently, Hannah helped the older woman ready herself for bed.

Lily's eyelids were already drooping. By

the time Hannah left the room she could hear the elderly lady's soft snore.

Ty was in the hallway.

"She's sleeping," Hannah informed him.

"That was fast. She hasn't had dinner yet."

"She was very tired."

Ty stared at her appraisingly, his dark eyes seeming to x-ray her soul. Hannah was afraid he could see right through to the events of yesterday. "Now would you tell me what's really going on? I come home and Irene and Danny are acting weird, Lily is so exhausted she doesn't even talk to me and I can see you're agitated. What went on while I was gone?"

At that moment, Danny and Irene mounted the stairs.

"Irene is going to read me a story," Danny announced. Both of them averted their eyes so they didn't have to look at Ty.

Talk about being bad liars! Hannah thought. They looked as if they were prevaricating about something even when they were telling the truth.

"We'd better go downstairs," Hannah suggested.

"Into my study, then."

She was going to lose her job; she *should*

lose it. She hadn't listened to Ty, and she'd taken Lily out and the poor woman had ended up overnight in the cardiac unit of the hospital. Hannah had probably set her back a month in her recovery time. What had she been thinking?

Of course, Hannah knew the answer. Lily's heart was going to break one way or the other, either from stress or because of her sadness over Clara.

Then she thought of the mess Trisha had gotten them into. She was still short almost two thousand dollars. The girl had purchased several items that couldn't be returned, Hannah had discovered. Not only did she have to find money for the delinquent mortgage, but also for credit cards with sky-high interest. Without a job there would be no way to catch up. With no way to catch up…Hannah couldn't go any further. If this snowballed and she lost the house, she had no idea where to turn. By the time they entered the study, Hannah had herself living in poverty, her home a shopping cart, her life over.

She sank onto one of the leather wing chairs across from his desk. It felt like butter, soft, pliable, rich. It would only take the price of *one* of these chairs to pay the mortgage.

Hannah was grateful when Ty switched on the gas fireplace. It was cool in the room and night was beginning to fall. Closeted with its thick drapes, endless bookshelves, dark wood and large, finely woven rugs the room felt like a private cocoon. It seemed as if she and Ty were on another planet, one all their own. She braced herself to be kicked off Planet Matthews very soon.

"When did Irene start reading to Danny?" Ty demanded. "And why is she here so late in the day? What caused my grandmother to be so exhausted that she couldn't even talk to me?"

"It's a long story."

"I've got all night, Hannah." He studied her face. "Maybe you should make some coffee. I have a hunch this might take a while."

She escaped to the kitchen and returned with a carafe and two mugs. She'd also done some baking earlier in the week, so the tray held chocolate-dipped biscotti and almond macaroons drizzled with chocolate.

The last supper, she thought morosely, her guilt genes firing on all cylinders.

He sat down behind the desk and waited.

"It all started yesterday, when Lily insisted she had to see Clara."

A groan escaped him. "I was afraid of that."

"She was relentless. She even quit eating. You know how she can be."

"Better than anyone. I hope you didn't humor her."

Hannah glanced at him, tears welling in her eyes. "I'm afraid I did."

"So you were at Clara's today?"

"Not exactly. We were there yesterday."

"Then where were you just now?" He looked puzzled.

"Seeing her friend upset Lily a good deal. I didn't like how she was behaving after we left. She'd become so agitated that I was afraid she might have a heart attack or a ministroke."

"Keep going." He sounded grim.

"So I took her to the emergency room. I thought it wouldn't hurt to play it safe. They did an EKG, which was normal, but they decided to keep her overnight wearing a monitor so they could watch her. It was just a precaution and I felt better that they did that. Lily's okay, just tired.

"In fact, her heart is very strong for her age. 'A remarkable specimen,' they called her, at least fifteen years younger than her actual age." She looked into his face, now creased with concern. "Ty, I'm giving you *good* news, not bad."

"She was in the hospital all night? And you didn't call me?"

"Actually, I did. You never picked up."

"There were no messages."

"I didn't want to leave one. I thought it was something you needed to hear directly from me."

"You make all sorts of decisions, don't you, Hannah?"

"I did my best."

"You promised me that you wouldn't take her out while I was gone."

"She was working herself into a frenzy! What was I supposed to do?"

"Call me."

"But you didn't answer!"

They could go around like this all night, Hannah thought.

"Tell me everything that happened—at Clara's, what made you take Lily to the hospital, what the doctor said." His blue eyes had grown inky and she didn't know how to read them.

"Nothing much has changed there," Hannah said wearily, sinking deep into the leather chair, wishing she could disappear into its depths. Truth be told, she yearned to vanish and not come back until her mortgage was paid and Ty wasn't scowling at her.

"Lily was very firm about being *alone* with her friend, so I had to respect that. I don't know what they discussed, but if Lily could have taken Clara home with her, she probably would have. She's convinced that we need to rescue Clara. She's obviously suffering from benign neglect because neither John nor his mother have any training or skills as a caregiver. Psychologically, it can't be good. Even Lily suggested a care facility of some kind. The emotional part of being old may be the most difficult—losing one's independence, one's mobility, one's friends."

"The last part is the hardest," Ty said softly. "I see that. It doesn't seem fair. But that doesn't negate the fact that Lily spent the night in a hospital."

"Look at it this way—if she was going to have trouble, we'd have nipped it in the bud. Better safe than sorry," she added brightly.

"Lily wore you down. Why should you be surprised that Lily could wear me down, too?"

"You're the expert, Hannah. You should

be able to take any pressure a patient puts on you and refuse to give in if those are your instructions."

"They weren't really reasonable instructions." She found herself terribly annoyed. "Lily isn't a prisoner here. She's clear and cognizant of everything. Surely she should have some say in her own life."

"Not when her ideas land her in the hospital."

"Oh, come on, that was a precaution. If I hadn't taken her to the hospital, you would have been mad at me then, too."

She should probably keep her mouth shut, Hannah realized. She hated arguing with him; she despised interacting with him like this, when she couldn't see the tender, funny side of him.

Still, she couldn't go without saying what she had to tell him. For Lily's sake, not his. "You're going overboard with her, Ty. She's a lot more resilient than you give her credit for being. You complain that your grandfather pampered her too much, yet you are doing exactly the same thing. Why shouldn't she push the edges of the envelope? She enjoys being indulged and cosseted. Why not find out how much pampering she can get? She's smart—savvy like a toddler who knows how to work his parents. Ask her. She'll tell you that herself."

He groaned and raked his fingers through his hair, a sure sign of his frustration. "I expected you to be more protective of her, after the types of things you've seen and know happen. You know I'll do anything to see that Lily is well taken care of."

She reached out a hand, wishing she could touch him, smooth the dark hair he'd rumpled. "All I'm saying is that you should ease up for your own sake and Lily's. Even Lily doesn't like to be coddled every moment. Let her get out and live her life."

The look he gave her could have cut diamonds. Then his expression softened. "You're probably right." He sighed. "I know the strength of Lily's will. I was just hoping that somehow you could find a way…"

Tears were running down her cheeks when she reached across the desk and grabbed his hand. "I'm so sorry."

Silently Ty stood up, came around to her side of the desk, took Hannah in his arms and let her cry. He rested his cheek on the crown of her head, smelling the fragrance of her shampoo, finding himself wanting to do whatever it took to make this woman happy.

Chapter Sixteen

She awoke late the next morning and scrambled out of bed. Danny was already dressed and eating breakfast with Irene when Hannah entered the kitchen.

"Hi, sleepyhead," he said with a grin. He jumped up, grabbed his backpack and headed for the door. "Josh's mom is giving me a ride to school today. He and I are going to feed the hamsters and the lizards before school 'cause it's our turn. See ya later, Mom." He breezed a kiss by Hannah's cheek and scooted out the door.

Hannah smiled, grateful that Danny had found a good friend. He'd been a little short on them at school lately.

"Did you sleep well, Hannah?" Irene asked

when Hannah walked into the kitchen. She handed her a cup of coffee.

"I remember seeing 4:00 a.m. on the clock."

"Must have been that kind of night. Mr. Matthews looked tired, too. 'Course he had to get up and catch a plane this morning. He left about the time I arrived."

Hannah was stunned. He hadn't told her he was leaving again. Of course, there'd been a lot of other things going on last night.

"Mr. Matthews asked me to stay with you while he's gone," Irene continued. "He said you probably would like a little time off. I'll be here all day, so feel free to relax. When you come back, I'll go get a bag with a night-gown and a change of clothes."

"How long will he be gone? Did he tell you?"

"Awhile, I think. Three days, maybe? He didn't sound quite sure. I suppose it depends on how things go business-wise."

Three days? It might have been three decades. The house didn't feel right without Ty in it—at least after last night when Ty had held her.

Later, Hannah peeked in on Lily to tell her she was taking the day off.

"Ty wasn't difficult with you, was he?"

Lily asked worriedly. "Don't pay any attention to him. His bark is much worse than this bite." Lily studied Hannah. "Oh, dear, he fussed at you, didn't he? I'll talk to him about it."

"He had every right to fuss. I took you out and you got upset and ended up in the hospital. Fine caregiver I am." *Besides, he comforted me far more than he fussed.*

"Nonsense. I wanted to go. I let myself get worked up. You did the only sensible thing by making sure I wasn't ill. He should give you a raise!"

"Well, he's gone again for a few days, so we'll just have to put this on the back burner. Irene is here today and I'm going to run errands." She leaned over and kissed the older woman on her papery-thin cheek. "Be good for her, okay?"

Lily's eyes danced. "I think I'll ask her if we can go to the park and ride the bumper cars!"

"Now I'm getting out of here for sure." Hannah waved goodbye over her shoulder as she left.

Tired from his second long, tedious day of meetings, Ty decided to eat in the hotel restaurant. He wasn't willing to tackle any more Los Angeles traffic. His brain and his body were tired. He'd signed his name on the dotted line for a lot of money, but he was accustomed to that. What he wasn't used to was spending his nights flopping around in his bed like a fish washed up on the beach.

It was Hannah's fault. She'd been haunting both his waking and sleeping thoughts. What was she doing tonight? Was she taking time off, as he'd hoped she would? She'd felt so remorseful and vulnerable in his arms that it would be impossible to stay upset with her. He had no doubt anymore that she would fight as much as he did for Lily's well-being.

And Danny. What was he doing? That little boy had really stolen his heart. He was hungry for a male influence. How could Ty be less than flattered that Danny had adopted him for that role? A smile touched the corners of his lips.

Then Ty realized that for the first time in a very long time he felt happy, truly happy. It occurred to him that he'd thought very little about Anita in the days since Hannah had crashed—literally—into his life.

Ty marveled at the thought. What had gotten into him?

Hannah, that's what.

Hannah decided that the first thing she should do was go to her house, check for unpaid bills, get online, check her account balance and see what they owed.

She pulled up to the house and parked, taking a few moments to stare at the small two-story house. Not seeing it every day was revealing, she realized. It would be ready for a paint job in a year or two. One of the shutters was crooked and a few shingles had blown off. The gray paint on the porch floor was peeling. It could use a face-lift. It wouldn't be cheap, but it would certainly help resale value.

She'd always seen her home through rose-colored glasses, but it wasn't really so different from all the other houses in the neighborhood. Only she knew that Steve had been the one to paint it, to dig and plant the flower beds, to put that ridiculous garden gnome in the front yard. But that was a long time ago. If she were to be honest, her memories no longer fed her as they once did. They'd become habit rather than comfort. Yet, without another relationship in her life, they'd been all she had.

But times had changed. Thanks to Ty Matthews, a part of her that had been dormant since Steve died was waking up. It was uncomfortable to admit it, considering that Ty was her employer, but perhaps she could love again.

As she walked up the sidewalk, she impulsively veered off the path and across the grass. She picked up the ludicrous gnome and carried it back to the car. She dusted it off and wrapped it in the blanket in the trunk and carefully placed it there. That treasure, at least, was a tangible memory.

Hannah opened the front door of the house with her key.

She hadn't been home much since Trisha and her friends had taken it over. It looked like there'd been a tornado through here; clothes everywhere, half-empty soda cans and shoes. The television, sans sound, was on. Hannah walked through the house. There was even uneaten food in pans on the stove. She opened the refrigerator to see mold on the food in her Tupperware.

Surely she'd raised Trisha better than this.

Hannah sank onto a kitchen chair before realizing it was suspiciously sticky.

Wearily she made her way to the rolltop desk in the living room where the bills were kept. She slid it open and stared in dismay. The new bills were there, all right, in a disorganized jumble, scattered among candy wrappers and crumpled receipts. She pulled up a chair and sat down to tackle the mess.

It took a half hour of sorting and organizing to find out that, although Trisha had finally paid last month's mortgage, there would be nothing left for the next payment, which was due only a week from now. In addition, she was behind on the utilities and had a significant amount on a credit card, including charges for restaurants, coffee shops and boutiques.

Trisha! Where did I go wrong?

She typed in her username and password for the bank, and her account popped onto the screen. She stared at it in disbelief. Something was wrong. There was enough money in the account to pay all the bills except for the balance of the credit card!

She opened the list of deposits and discovered the reason for the flush of money.

Tyler Matthews had paid her in advance

for the upcoming month. There it was—two payments of the same amount where one should be. She stared dumbly at the figure. The money would get her up-to-date again. It would give her time to put the brakes on her sister's irresponsibility. *It...it had to be a mistake.*

She hadn't earned the money yet. She needed to give it back.

It was a pleasant, if fleeting, moment, thinking she had a way to undo Trisha's irresponsibility—but it shouldn't be at Ty's expense.

The upstairs wasn't quite as disorganized and cluttered as the downstairs, Hannah thought gratefully. The girls' rooms were tidy and the bathroom was reasonably clean. She noticed that the hallway walls were scuffed and could use a coat of paint. The overhead light was the old-fashioned, open kind that collected both flies and dust. It needed a cleaning right now and should probably be replaced. The bathroom tile had seen better days, too. The woodwork should be refinished sometime and the carpet was showing its age.

She was seeing the place with new eyes, Hannah realized. She'd always viewed it as the precious home she and Steven had shared. But it was only a house, one like any other. If she lost it, if that was God's will, then she would accept that.

She'd been hanging on in her mind, thinking she couldn't survive without this place that housed the memories of her past, but she was finally seeing that it wasn't so. This was a house, a thing, a material possession. It was as if God was saying to her, "Depend on Me, not a house, not a job, not an object. Only Me."

"Only You, Lord," she murmured aloud. "It's all gone or going, Lord."

Suddenly, Hannah's heart felt lighter, as if the burden of the world had been lifted.

Chapter Seventeen

In the end, Hannah paid off what she could, including the minimum on the credit card. She would tell Ty about the overpayment and that she hadn't used the money. Maybe she could put the house on the market. If it sold quickly, she might escape foreclosure. She was a woman who had always paid her debts and she didn't want to stop now. She'd have to start looking for an apartment.

With most of the day still free, she found a cardboard box in the garage and carried it into the attic. She opened a large trunk, one that had once belonged to her parents, and started to sort through it. She found sweaters she wouldn't wear again, shoes that had never been comfortable, favorite blouses she'd outgrown and even a box of costume jewelry she'd collected over the years. She put it all into the cardboard box and sealed the lid with packing tape. She put that box by the front door, got another from the garage and continued to sort.

By the time Trisha arrived at home, there were seven filled boxes by the door.

She found Hannah in the attic, weeding out Christmas ornaments.

"Han? What are you doing?"

"Getting rid of a few things. You don't still want this Christmas teddy bear, do you? Some child would enjoy it."

"My bear? Of course I want it." Trisha dropped onto her knees on the floor beside Hannah.

"I've put some boxes in your room that have your things in them. You can go through those and get rid of what you don't want. I plan to work here for a day or two. Then I'll call The Salvation Army to pick them up."

"Why are you doing this? I don't want to get rid of anything."

Hannah turned to face her. "We may be moving from this house, Trisha. I'm not sure, but it is a possibility. I think it would be good to sort through our possessions now, just in case. Besides, we're not using anything up here. Think of the people who could enjoy what we aren't using. Some people have nothing and we have so much."

She skewered Trisha with a gaze. "Like all those things you purchased with the credit card the other day, after you said you wouldn't use it anymore. You promised."

"It was just a few things. I thought since you had a job it wouldn't matter."

"Little things add up. I paid the minimum balance. You'll have to come up with the rest."

Trisha looked dumbfounded.

Hannah heard the firmness and resolve in her own voice. This was the right thing to do. She was sure of it.

"It's a lot of money!"

"I thought it was just 'a few things.'"

"It was a few things when you were paying for it, I suppose, but a lot of money when I have to pay for it," Trisha admitted guiltily. She had the grace to blush.

"Trisha, the fact of the matter is, you didn't keep your promise. You didn't pay the bills," Hannah said bluntly. "We've fallen behind. If I can't pull us out, we may not keep the house if it becomes too big a burden."

"But it's our home!" Trisha wailed, as if finally realizing just how serious her sister was.

"We were living close to the bone and—"

"And I wasted the money you had? I didn't think it was really that bad, Hannah. You have a job."

"I tried to keep it from you so you wouldn't worry. I should have been talking to you all along, instead of trying to protect you. You didn't know exactly how month-to-month our existence has been. You realized some of it, I know, but not the full extent. But what's happened has happened. We'll just go forward from here."

"So are you really serious about getting rid of stuff?"

"It's just stuff, Trisha. We don't need it. God is enough."

When Ty returned home from his business trip, he got a tongue-lashing the likes of which he hadn't had since he'd saved up his lunch money to buy an iguana and bring it home to his grandparents. He'd not considered the fact that Lily was paralyzed with fear at the sight of lizards.

He'd figured Lily must really love him

after that, because she did allow him to keep Iggie, albeit in the potting shed in the backyard. She'd been delighted, however, when he took Iggie to school and started housing him in the classroom.

This time, however, it was all about Hannah.

"You took Hannah to task because *I* insisted we go to Clara's? She took wonderful care of me. I never would have gone to the doctor under my own steam. It seems to me you're angry with Hannah for doing her job!"

"I realize that, Gram, but you know she really shouldn't have taken you out when I asked her not to. Besides, it's all settled. We're okay." *More than okay.*

"And that's another thing! Who appointed you as my keeper, young man? I'm perfectly able to make my own decisions. My mind is clear!"

"I'm not debating that, Gram." Arguing with Lily was like trying to tame the wind. He never won. "I assumed you *wanted* me to watch out for you. Ever since Grandfather died, that's what I've thought you wanted. I know that's what *he* wanted."

Lily softened then. "I believe I did need a keeper back then. Your grandfather and I had a wonderful marriage. He wanted to pamper me and I let him. It was actually him who started it—and I loved being treated with such tenderness."

She looked suddenly sad and it pierced Ty's heart.

"But I see now that I continued accepting—and expecting—the same from you. It wasn't fair, Ty. I'm sorry."

An apology from his grandmother. It made Ty uneasy. He'd never seen her like this before. Hannah had changed all the dynamics in this house since she'd come.

"Hannah is a gem, Ty. Frankly, she'd make someone a fine granddaughter-in-law. You'll be long in the tooth pretty soon. Maybe you should think about..."

He threw up his hands. "Gram, please don't sharpen your matchmaking skills on me."

Lily stopped talking and smiled serenely. "Oh, darling, don't be so grim. Lighten up." She put her hand out to touch his cheek.

Ty didn't realize until much, much later that he'd failed to extract a promise from Lily not to meddle.

* * *

Hannah went outside and sat on the front steps to wait for Danny to arrive home from school.

She was mentally making plans for them to go to a late-afternoon movie or to the park, whichever Danny preferred, when the bus pulled up. The doors opened and Danny exited.

She opened her mouth to speak but closed it again. Her son's shoulders were slumped, his footsteps were heavy and he appeared to have been crying. She hurried toward him as the bus pulled away.

"Honey…"

"Go away, Mom."

Stunned, she stared at him. He'd never spoken to her like that before.

"What's wrong, Danny? I'm your mother—you can talk to me."

"You're a girl. You wouldn't get it."

"Try me. What happened today?"

He looked at her and she could see tear tracks on his cheeks—and the beginning of a black eye.

"It's guy stuff, Mom. *Guy* stuff."

"Danny, I insist…"

He relented. "I got picked on by one of the big kids on the bus. He hit me so I shoved him back and *I* got in trouble. It's not even fair!" Without another word, he went inside.

Hannah had anticipated that this would happen, that someday Danny would need someone other than her to talk to. How she wished Steve were here right now.

Her stomach hurt. *God is enough. He is enough.*

She reiterated that over and over, supremely grateful that He *was* enough because everything else in her life seemed to be falling apart.

Chapter Eighteen

The next day, Danny's eye was still painfully angry-looking and puffed half shut. He was a silent little shadow around the house, reluctant even to visit with Lily—who would no doubt drill him about what had happened. He watched television every free moment, his eyes fixed on the screen so intently that Hannah suspected he was using it as a means to escape talking to her.

Finally, it got to be too much. She needed to talk to someone who had been a little boy once and could relate to Danny.

Ty was holed up in his office when Hannah found him. She knocked on the door and entered, almost before he had time to respond to her knock. She straightened her shoulders, thrust her chin forward and marched toward his desk. "Have you seen Danny lately?"

"No. He was in bed when I came home. What's up with my buddy?"

"Then you haven't seen his black eye?"

Ty looked surprised.

"It's a shiner. A big one. He hasn't even been in to see Lily because I'm sure he's trying to hide it from her. She'd ask him a million questions."

"What happened?"

"A boy picked on him on the bus and they got into a fight. He doesn't want to talk about it. He says it's because I'm a 'girl.' I thought, maybe, if you could, if you thought it would help, since his father is gone—"

"You want me to talk to him man-to-man. To see if I can find out what's going on?"

Relief made her legs watery. "Yes. I don't know where else to turn. I certainly haven't cultivated a lot of men friends who could step in except...you."

"He probably doesn't want to upset you with whatever the fight was about."

"But he's upsetting me *more* by not talking. Danny and I have always shared everything."

"Little boys take a lot of things on their

shoulders that they shouldn't. I should know. I'm sorry you didn't tell me right away. I'll talk to him, although I can't make any guarantees."

The release she felt was monumental. She didn't realize, until that moment, how stiffly she'd been holding her entire body. She melted backward into the chair.

"You should have asked me sooner. I had my share of black eyes as a kid. Every one was either very traumatic or a badge of honor. I get it completely."

"I didn't want to bother you."

"No bother. Danny's a great little boy. If he needs someone to talk to, I'm happy to be the one." Ty rolled his pen in his fingers. "I thought you knew by now you can come to me with anything. If you can't get into trouble when Lily ends up in the emergency room, a black eye should be nothing. Besides, I've been looking for an excuse to take that boy under my wing."

Hannah interpreted that to mean *this boy needs a father figure*. She couldn't have agreed more.

"It's not really Danny that's been the problem, it's been me." She looked at him steadily. "I saw that you put extra money in my account." Hannah dropped her head. "I'm ashamed to admit it, but for a moment I actually considered using it to pay my bills. But that wouldn't have been right. I'll write you a check to pay you back. You can give it to me next month—after I've earned it."

The look he gave her was unexpected—amazement, disbelief, even incredulity. "You didn't spend it to pay your bills? That's what I put it there for!"

Now it was Hannah's turn to be surprised. "But why? How did you even know I was in trouble?"

Ty raked his fingers through his dark hair, leaving it ruffled and appealing. "Because I overheard you and your sister talking while I was sitting out on the porch at your place. The windows were open so it was difficult not to hear your conversation. I heard Trisha admit she'd run up other bills and didn't have the money. I doubted she could make enough no matter how many part-time jobs she took on, so I put the money in your account to help you out."

Ty pushed himself away from the desk. "I wanted you to use it to get caught up. Consider it an advance or even a loan if you must, but just use it."

Hannah's world suddenly shifted and a verse in Isaiah came to mind. *Fear not, for I am with you... I will help you.* God had been helping her all the time. Her worry had blinded her. She should have trusted Him—and Ty—from the beginning.

As Ty rose, Hannah jumped to her feet. Full of gratitude and not thinking straight, she barreled into him and gave him a hug. "Thank you, thank you, thank you!"

The feel of his hard, broad chest and the warmth of his body drew her even closer. She clung to him fiercely.

She felt his lips on her forehead, her cheek, her lips and she willingly responded with a kiss of her own and was lost in Ty's embrace.

Later, after Ty had left to find Danny, Hannah sat dazedly on a leather chair in Ty's office. She lifted her fingers to her lips. She could still feel the warmth of him there. He'd made her head swim with that single kiss and suddenly her world felt more topsy-turvy than ever.

If he'd ever seen a child more miserable, Ty thought, he couldn't remember it. Danny was squirming uncomfortably on the living room couch.

He might as well cut to the chase, Ty thought. "Where'd you get the shiner, Danny?"

The boy looked dismayed. "On the bus."

"From who?"

"A kid."

"Which kid? And why'd he do it?"

"Kevin. He lives down the street."

Ty knew the boy well. Kevin was an unpleasant child at best, a spoiled brat at worst. More than once Ty had found him skulking outside the house looking in the windows. His parents were notorious snoops in the neighborhood, and apparently the kid had inherited the gene.

"We got in a fight because he said something bad about my mom." Danny brightened for a second. "I think the black eye I gave him is bigger."

Ty suppressed a smile.

"He said she was a 'squatter' and that she took this job so she could get close to you. He said his mother told him so." Danny's eyes grew wide. "What's a squatter?"

The mother again. That woman had caused more neighborhood squabbles over the years than...what was it that Lily always said?

Oh, yes, more squabbles than Carter's has liver pills.

"A squatter is someone who is living on someone else's property and hasn't been invited to live there."

"But we were invited, right?"

"Absolutely."

"And why would my mom *try* to get close to you? She can stand by you anytime she wants!"

Ty loved the innocence of childhood. Little did Danny know that the neighbor woman in question was dying to catch Tyler in some embarrassing act. Ty had once discovered her husband turning back the odometer on a car they were about to sell and chastised him for it. She'd hated him ever since, and now her son was taking it out on Danny. Ty almost felt sorry for Kevin, being raised by a woman like that.

"Danny, your mom was not only invited to come here, she was *hired* to be here and to be in touch with me about my grandmother's health and well-being. She wouldn't be doing her job if we weren't in conversation about that. Not only is what that little boy said false, it's hurtful."

"So it was okay that I took a swing at him?" For the first time, Danny looked hopeful.

It must have been a heavy burden to carry, Ty thought, fighting for his mother's honor and then not being able to tell her about it. Poor kid.

"It wasn't okay to take a swing, no. But I understand why you did it. I think you should tell your mother what happened, Danny."

Danny sighed and stood up. "Okay, but what if I get punished?"

"You won't."

Danny slunk out of the room, feet dragging and shoulders drooping.

It occurred to Ty that he felt unduly satisfied with himself. It was a good feeling to help guide a child, to point a boy in the direction he should go. It felt...*fatherly.*

That thought hit Ty like a blow. How had he gone from being a man who avoided women to one who liked to help Hannah and her son?

God had slipped something in his life when he wasn't looking, that was for sure.

Within fifteen minutes, Hannah was in Ty's office, her eyes brimming with tears. "Thank you. Danny just told me what happened. Poor baby, keeping all that to himself. I can't thank you enough." She leaned forward, her expression so earnest and so grateful that it tugged at his heartstrings.

"Anytime," Ty said, realizing how completely he meant it. That impulsive kiss had shaken him to his core. Hannah St. James and her little boy had wormed their way into his heart.

Chapter Nineteen

Hannah caught Ty in the hallway as he was about to enter Lily's room. She silently crooked her finger and beckoned him to the other end of the hallway.

"What's up?" he asked.

Hannah felt her face redden. She was acting like a lovesick teenager and told herself to snap out of it. She couldn't come apart at the seams every time she was near Ty. She'd be a blathering mess. "I'd like to talk about the situation with Clara."

He gestured her toward an arrangement of chairs and a small table by the window at the end of the hall. "Let's sit down and you can tell me."

Hannah glanced toward Lily's room. "Maybe we should go to your office. Just in case. I don't want Lily to overhear us."

"Good idea."

He put his hand at the small of Hannah's back as she opened the door to his office, and stepped inside after her.

His touch made her skin grow warm.

She sank into a big leather chair and he sat across from her. Here they were again, holed up together in this dark, intimate room.

"I think Lily is correct. We need to help Clara. From what Lily says, things are deteriorating over there. Clara could have a much better quality of life."

"What do you suggest?"

He was clenching and unclenching his fists, Hannah noticed, a sure sign that what had been an academic question in his mind was becoming a very personal one.

"Before we do anything else, I think it would be lovely if we took Lily and Clara out for lunch. It would be good for both of them. It would also give us an opportunity to talk to her away from her sister's place."

"I guess we have to start somewhere. Where do you suggest we take them?"

"I think they'd both love a visit to The Farmhouse. How about you?"

"Perfect." Ty appeared pleased by the idea.

"We can take Danny with us. Maybe we can get in a game of miniature golf."

Hannah felt happiness surge through her, grateful that Tyler had thought of Danny.

"Great idea. I think Clara will enjoy him, too. A small boy always brings life to a gathering. Not always the right kind, of course."

"He's a great kid, Hannah. Lily loves him. I'm already dreading when the time comes for you and Danny to move back home."

You and me both, Hannah thought to herself.

Both Clara and Lily had dressed up for their outing. Clara had worked hard on her silver hair, smoothing it into a flattering chignon. Lily's cheeks were bright with blush.

Ty suppressed a smile. His fondness for his grandmother's friend was growing. Lily had been so independent and vibrant until she broke her foot that Ty had never considered her old. Now it was on his mind all the time.

Ironically, he'd begun thinking of his own age, too. Who would he have to grow old with? That idea hadn't even occurred to him until recently. He knew now that he didn't want to grow old alone.

When Hannah turned to smile at him, it

took Ty aback just to look at her. She was beautiful today, casual in jeans and a pink shirt that shouldn't have gone well with her rusty-red hair, but it did. She was free of makeup and he could see the light freckles on the bridge of her nose. He liked a woman comfortable with herself. Her hair was pulled into a high, wild ponytail and bounced when she moved her head.

"There's as much squealing and laughing back there," Ty tipped his head to the back of the vehicle where the ladies and Danny were, "as a bunch of teenagers at a slumber party."

"They're happy to be out and to be together."

Ty, in a low voice, asked the question that had been eating at him. "What are we going to do, Hannah? It devastates Lily to know Clara isn't well cared for."

Hannah didn't have time to answer, however. By then they had arrived at The Farmhouse.

"Tyler," Lily said imperiously as the ladies were waiting for tea after their lunch, "Clara and I will sit here and visit while you take this boy outside and play golf. He's been an angel and deserves a treat. You know how much you loved that as a child."

"Is that an order, Gram?"

"Yes. And if we get bored, we'll ask for help to get to the gift shop."

"No doubt," Ty said wearily. Lily could talk feathers off a duck. It would be easy for her to find assistance. "How about it, Danny?"

The little boy jumped to his feet.

"And take Hannah with you. We'll be fine without her." With that, Lily turned back to her friend.

As they walked outside, with Danny dancing along beside them, Hannah said, "I've become dispensable, I see."

She actually sounded hurt at the idea.

"Don't worry. When she's exhausted and needs to get to bed tonight, you'll be essential again. Take it from one who knows."

Hannah had a difficult time concentrating. Ty didn't look like the other men on the mini-golf course. They and their children, vacationers, no doubt, were in jeans and brightly colored T-shirts. Ty wore a suit and tie more appropriate for a conference room than a children's playground. In a crisp charcoal-colored suit and tie and a shirt that was so pale a pink that it looked almost white, he was, frankly, gorgeous. The smooth, athletic way he moved was sinuous and strong. Plus, he managed to make putting a golf ball into a fake mouse hole on the course look elegant.

In fact, more than once Danny had to say to her, "Mom, pay attention! It's your turn."

Hannah hoped Ty hadn't noticed her dreamy, adolescent behavior. She'd never been this way, even as a teenager. Ty had awakened these feelings in her.

Danny trounced them at golf. Of course, Hannah knew she and Ty hadn't exactly been paying attention. Every time their eyes met, it affected their play.

The ladies were waiting for them on the porch of The Farmhouse when they were finished playing. It was remarkable how happy they looked.

Clara couldn't stop thanking them on the way home. She had tears in her eyes. It hurt Hannah to leave her behind.

Lily, too, was appreciative.

"This is the best day I've had since I tripped over that dog and broke my foot," she proclaimed.

Hannah turned around to ask her, "Are you tired, Lily?"

But the older woman was already asleep.

Chapter Twenty

Lily and Danny were up to something, Hannah realized, but she had no idea what.

She could hear them giggling in Lily's bedroom, but they grew silent every time Hannah entered. She'd even tried eavesdropping from her own room by listening through the door to the adjoining bath, but she guessed they were holding a bath towel to the door to muffle the sound.

The very thought of them conspiring made her uneasy. Those two quick minds could hatch plans that could have her tearing her hair out.

Irene seemed to know they were up to something, but her lips were sealed. When Hannah asked her what was going on, Irene, eyes twinkling, had made as if to zip her lips with her thumb and forefinger.

Reluctantly, Hannah made her way to Ty's office.

He was working at home today and didn't like to be disturbed, but she had strict instructions to keep him apprised of what Lily was doing. She stood before the vast wooden door to the office and knocked.

She thought once again of how this house with its ten-foot coffered ceilings, eight-foot-tall windows, vast stretches of hardwood and Oriental rugs that probably cost a year of her mortgage payments each differed from her own modest dwelling. With every passing day, she found herself caring less and less about her house. There was immense freedom in that, she'd discovered. She'd placed far too much importance on it in the past.

It also helped that she and Danny had no extra living expenses. Food was provided, as was gas for her car, and Ty had even paid for her license tabs because she was living under his roof when they came due. She wished she could buy better clothing, but because of her small size, she did fairly well at the sale racks of discount stores.

Only last week, Tyler had complimented her on a sleek emerald dress that Hannah had found discarded and wadded in a lump in the dressing room of a store. The final sale price had been fifty percent off fifteen dollars. After laundering and restitching the hem, it had turned into a perfectly nice dress that highlighted her red-gold hair.

Those thoughts only reminded her that she needed to talk to Trisha again, to see if she was keeping up with the bills. She knew her sister was working hard. Trisha's roommate Jane had assured Hannah that her new boyfriend, Jason, who Hannah had finally met, wasn't contributing to the problem. Apparently, he had more than one job himself, besides school, and would get on Trisha's case if she tried to slack off. That was the kind of man her sister needed, Hannah thought grimly—one who didn't let her slip back into her immature habits.

"Come in," Ty called.

When she entered, he was standing, sorting through a four-drawer file cabinet. He wore casual trousers and a blue cotton shirt. When he turned to look at her she saw that the blue of his shirt made the color of his eyes even brighter and more piercing. Those baby blues alone were enough to make a woman weak in the knees.

"Yes?"

She slumped into a chair. By now, they'd had enough of these heart-to-hearts about Lily, Danny, Clara and Trisha and her finances that she was no longer intimidated by the vastness of the room and its furniture.

"I think we have trouble, but I don't know what it is."

Ty scowled. "Lily was so tired after her day out that I thought she was laying low. What is she up to?"

"What are *they* up to, you mean. She and Danny have been terribly secretive. Every time I walk in the room they both get very quiet and look delighted when I leave again. When you were a boy, did she include you in the schemes she hatched?"

Ty thought about it, walked to his desk and dropped into the chair across from her. "Always." He rested his forehead on his hand as if he'd gotten a sudden headache.

"I can't wait until she's back on her own two feet and living in her own house again."

Hannah's spirits sank a little. She understood what he was saying, but that would mean she'd no longer be needed here. Even if they did decide to keep her on in some capacity, it would be in Lily's home, not Ty's. She felt an empty spot within just thinking about it. She'd come to look forward to her time with Ty.

"Is there any particular reason for stirring the pot?"

"No, nothing. It's a very ordinary week." She cocked her head and thought about it. "Except it is my birthday tomorrow. Maybe she and Danny are planning a cake and candles." Her frown cleared. "I could handle that."

"Your birthday?" Ty asked. "Do you have plans to celebrate?"

"I thought I might put a candle in my oatmeal in the morning."

"Very funny."

"My husband always used to make a big deal of that day. I haven't done anything special in years. Less sad, I suppose."

"That's why you *should* have a celebration. He wanted it for you when he was alive. I'm sure he'd want it for you now."

"Maybe you're right. Steve always wanted me happy. And he loved birthdays."

"You loved him a lot, didn't you?" Ty said softly.

He was so compassionate that Hannah was touched. "With all my heart."

Sometimes when he looked at her she felt as though he were seeing her soul. Hannah twiddled with the chain she wore around her neck. "You know, I've been a widow almost three times as long as I was married." She felt a flush flood her cheeks.

"How do you feel about that?"

His question startled her. No one had ever asked her that. She realized she'd never even asked *herself* that.

"I…I'm not sure. It sounds like a long time, doesn't it?" She chewed her lip thoughtfully. "Sometimes I feel like I've been alone forever."

"Are you planning to do anything to change that?"

His voice was bland, but the question sent up flares in her mind.

"What could I do?" She suddenly felt off-kilter.

"Get out more. Live your life. Make friends."

"I must look like a real loser to you, Ty."

"Not at all. In every aspect of your life— except your driving, of course—I think you're a winner. I find it odd that you don't realize it yourself. It's not my business, Hannah, but maybe it's time for you to have some fun in your life."

"What with raising Danny and Trisha, my sister's financial immaturity, paying the bills, losing my job…"

"My point exactly." Ty gave her an enigmatic look and shrugged those wide shoulders of his.

"Maybe *you* should take some of your own advice," she pointed out bluntly.

"Touché."

She was still considering her conversation with Ty at bedtime. He asked too many questions for which she had no answers. How *did* she feel about her widowhood after so many years? She'd tried not to think too much about it until she'd met Ty. She slept restlessly that night and woke up feeling ragged and weary. It was Ty's fault, Hannah decided. He asked too many questions.

The next morning when Ty returned from his run Danny, Irene and Lily, in her wheelchair, were in the kitchen.

His grandmother was managing to leave her room more often lately, probably because Hannah insisted on having her do therapy exercises three times a day. She was almost back to her old self.

"What's going on here?"

"We're making breakfast for Mom," Danny said proudly. "Did you get the flowers?"

"I did. Three dozen. I'll put them on the table. I also got a card. I'll sign it from Lily and me." If anyone deserved flowers, it was Hannah. He didn't feel the least bit guilty about not solving her curiosity of last night.

"Don't put my name on the card. *I* already have a present for her," Lily told him.

"Shh," Irene said. "I hear her coming down the stairs. Everyone in their seats. Sing when she walks in."

Doing as they were told, they scrambled into chairs and began singing when a disheveled Hannah stepped into the kitchen. She clapped her hands to her face and a sweet smile spread over her features.

"So this is what you were planning."

"Irene made your favorites, Mom. Baked French toast, turkey sausage and yogurt parfaits." Danny patted the chair beside his. "Sit here."

Irene began to serve, while Lily regaled them with a story about the birthday party Ty had organized for her when he was Danny's age. Ty had thought that Lily would love having a party with all his young friends, and Lily had found herself playing softball and ruining her outfit when she slid into third base.

That was, Lily reminded them all, when she was just a spring chick—still in her 60s.

"Now it's time for my present," Danny announced. "You're going to love it, Mom. Lily helped me with it, but it was my idea."

The child jumped up and ran to the far end of the room, opened a cupboard and pulled out a wicker suitcase. It was obviously heavy, but he was determined to present it to his mother by himself. He dragged it across the kitchen and set it at Hannah's feet.

"What's this?"

Danny hopped on his tiptoes excitedly. "Open it, Mom. Open it!"

Ty felt his curiosity increase. If Lily was involved in this, that small case could hold just about anything.

Hannah lifted it to the table and slowly opened her gift.

It wasn't a suitcase at all, Ty realized. It was a picnic basket. A packed picnic basket. There were plastic containers labeled *chicken, potato salad, pickles, strawberries* and *dessert*. At least that was all he could see. The thing was chockablock full.

"How lovely!" Hannah picked up a brightly colored plastic plate. "You and I are going on a picnic."

"Yeah. Lily said the mountains are great and that she and Ty used to go there." Danny's smile was wide.

"You want to go on a picnic today?" Hannah looked confused. "What about school?"

"I thought you could let me skip school today. Please? Your birthday is special."

She looked at him sadly. "But yesterday you brought home a note from your teacher saying that today everyone would be testing, remember? You can't miss that."

Danny's eager expression dissolved. "That's today?"

"I didn't mention it, honey, because I thought it wouldn't matter. I'm sorry. We can go on our picnic this weekend. Maybe after church?"

"But the basket is full *now!*"

"I have an idea," Lily said. "This way your mom can have two birthdays. Ty needs a break as much as you do, Hannah. Why don't the two of you go and enjoy the picnic?

"Irene will pack another lunch when you

and Danny want to go. We want you to have a wonderful day. Isn't that right, Danny?"

Hannah saw Danny relax. Poor little guy. He'd worked so hard on this only to have it fail over something he didn't anticipate.

"Ty, will you?" Danny's eyes were so pleading that Ty would have agreed to any of Lily's machinations. Besides, spending the day with Hannah was appealing.

"I can swing it."

"But you have so much work to do," Hannah protested. "You don't have to—"

"Where did you plan to go on your picnic, Danny?" Ty asked.

Before the child could answer, Lily jumped in smoothly. "I think the two of you should go to the mountains. Then Danny can take his mother to the park just as he'd planned."

Ty wondered fleetingly if Lily had somehow finagled all this, but he discarded the notion. She had, however, definitely taken advantage of the moment.

The clouds on Danny's face fled. "Two picnics? That's even better, right, Mom?"

He looked so hopeful that it nearly broke Hannah's heart. "The best, sweetheart. Twice as wonderful as one picnic." She glanced uncertainly at Ty but couldn't read his features.

Hannah jumped to her feet and made her way around the table, giving each person a grateful hug. "I'll go upstairs and get showered right away." She pressed a kiss onto the top of Danny's head and hurried away.

"Are you mad at me?" Danny's eyes were wide as he addressed Ty. "I really forgot about the testing."

"No, Danny, I'm not mad. It will be a privilege to take your mom on a birthday picnic." If he were to admit how he really felt about the change in plans, he'd be smiling himself silly.

Chapter Twenty-One

Ty backed his BMW convertible out of the garage. Top down, music playing on the radio, he yelled teasingly, "I've got a need for speed. Hop in." He flashed a boyish grin. Only one word came to Hannah's mind. *Hunk.*

She put the picnic basket in the backseat, rounded the silver car and jumped in.

They caught I-70 and wound their way toward and up the mountain. The slopes grew gradually steeper and the landscape greener. She could even feel the air change. The higher they climbed, the more lighthearted Hannah became.

Impulsively, she put her hands in the air. "Wheee!"

"What kind of driver am I if you think you're on a roller coaster?" Ty asked with a grin.

"This is as close as I've come to a roller coaster for a while. Trisha and I went on one once and I threw up all over her."

"Then you are wise to err on the side of caution."

The air grew cooler and thinner as they climbed and Hannah's excitement grew.

"I love to come up here. It's so beautiful and so grand," she said. "It's a snapshot of what our Creator can do."

"When I was a kid, we came to the mountains a lot. My grandfather always said he could have been a mountain man given half a chance. He was a big, strong fellow."

"Not exactly a place for Lily, however."

Ty laughed out loud. "Now there's a picture." He turned to look at her. "Is there someplace special you want to go?"

"Take me to the place you and your grandparents used to go for picnics."

"It's been so many years. We spent a lot of time around Evergreen. If you take this road far enough, you'll end up in Vale."

"Do you ski?" Hannah asked.

"Yes, when I have time. I'm particularly fond of black diamonds."

"And I'm on the other end of the spectrum. Give me a bunny hill any day. Steve and I never had a lot of extra money to spend, so my abilities are pretty limited. My parents were excellent skiers, though."

"Then someday I'll teach you."

Pleased, Hannah closed her eyes against the sunlight and enjoyed the feel of the wind whipping through her hair.

She must have dozed off because when she awoke, the car was parked and Ty was spreading a quilt on the ground beneath a canopy of trees. The picnic basket was at his feet.

She stretched sinuously as she got out of the car and walked toward him. "I don't know why I'm so sleepy. I didn't think I was that far behind on rest."

"You're relaxing. We have all day. Take a siesta if you like." Ty sat down on the blanket and pulled the basket into the center of it. "It's your birthday."

Her curiosity got the best of her. "Let's see what Irene put in that basket."

As she was removing containers from the basket, Ty reached for the largest one. "If this is Irene's fried chicken, we're in luck. Best I've ever tasted." He popped the lid to reveal crusty golden pieces. "Perfect."

There was a mound of potato salad, crisp

pickle wedges and fresh strawberries with a creamy fruit dip.

They filled their plates and ate in comfortable silence.

"This mountain air makes me ravenous," Hannah helped herself to a third piece of chicken and another scoop of salad. "This is embarrassing. I usually don't eat like a hard laborer."

"I'd think something was wrong with you if you didn't." Ty stretched out along one side of the blanket, one hand propped beneath his head and the other forking food into his mouth. He looked like a model for a Ralph Lauren photo shoot—a sophisticated man of the manor lounging against the lush, green background of his estate.

How had she found herself in such close proximity to such a nearly perfect specimen of manhood after all these long, lean years of widowhood? Hannah wondered this as she dug deeper into the basket.

"This is still half-full. What else could Irene have packed in here?" She lifted a 9 X 13 pan from the flat bottom of the basket and carefully lifted the lid.

"Chocolate cake!"

Happy Birthday, Hannah! was emblazoned

in pale buttercream frosting across the chocolate fudge.

"And more chocolate. The whole bottom of the basket is covered with candy bars."

"Danny's contribution, no doubt. He knows my weaknesses."

"You have weaknesses?" Ty acted shocked. "Other than your driving abilities, I mean."

She swatted at him playfully. "You should act more surprised that I have strengths," she teased.

"I have no doubt of that, Hannah. In fact, I…" He bit off whatever he was about to say and instead pointed at the cake. "Cut me a slice of that, will you?"

She probably had chocolate all over herself and she didn't care. The nice thing about Ty—and something she'd appreciated in Steve—was that he liked her without artifice.

When she'd announced once that she was going to the drug store to refill some prescriptions for Lily and buy herself some makeup, he'd asked her why. "You look good the way you are. Don't mess it up."

He'd blushed and backtracked immediately. "Sorry, I didn't mean to tell you what to do. I just think being natural… Go ahead, don't listen to me."

In the end, all she'd purchased was some soft pink lip gloss and a new clip with which to tie back her hair. If Ty, Danny, Lily and Irene all liked her the way she was, why, as Ty had said, should she mess it up?

"Want to take a walk?" Ty inquired.

"Actually, what I'd love to do is wade in that brook." She pointed to the burbling stream a few yards behind them.

"The rocks are slippery."

"I brought pool shoes along. They have excellent treads."

"And I have tennis shoes in the trunk that will grip the rock. I guess we're all set then." He rose languidly and held out his hand to her. "Let's go."

They each changed shoes, then his hand engulfed her smaller one as he led her toward the water. She felt delicate and feminine next to him. Oddly, she also felt safe. That was how it had been with Steve. As if nothing could touch her when she was with him.

The water, which was mountain runoff, felt colder than she'd expected as it swirled around Hannah's ankles. Once, a small silvery fish swam over the top of her foot and she would have sworn another nibbled at her toe. She romped and frolicked like an otter until she felt the bottoms of her rolled-up pants getting damp. Her already-curly hair was a mass of red ringlets. And if she was a playful otter, then Ty was a big, calm golden retriever, patient, tolerant, vigilant, watching her with pleasure. They hiked in the stream as far as they could before growing too cold and turning around and returning to their picnic spot. He kept her hand tight in his.

She dropped onto the blanket spread on a bed of pine needles, puffing. "That was hard work, keeping my balance in all that water!"

"Tired?" Ty took off his wet shoes and squeezed the water out of his socks.

"I am. Maybe I will take that siesta after all."

"You do that." He dropped onto the blanket beside her and to her surprise, pulled her close and dropped a kiss on her forehead. "Happy birthday, Hannah."

"Very," she purred as she curled on one corner of the coverlet and laid her head on her folded hands—and then nothing.

He watched her sleep. She made little faces as she catnapped, smiling softly, wiggling her nose, once even arching her eyebrows. It was as entertaining as a dozen movies. She reminded him of Danny as she slept, a be-guiling innocence radiated from her.

Hannah captivated him. She was steady and strong for Lily, understanding and help-ful to Irene, patient and loving with Danny and far more compassionate and tolerant with Trisha than Ty thought he could ever be in her situation. And uncomplaining. Whatever any of them dished out, including him, she took in her stride. She was fragile and bold, delicate and sturdy, funny and serious, a most complex personality.

He shouldn't try to analyze it, but that was easier than admitting the realization that he was falling in love.

He groaned a little and she squirmed in her sleep before going still again.

Anita was still there, drifting on the edges of his consciousness, but he'd thought about her less lately. It was as if she was releas-ing the hold she had on him. But he knew it wasn't that. Anita would never have wished for him to grieve as he had, to shut off that part of his life. She'd loved him too much. He'd done that to himself.

And now there was Hannah.

They'd had an inauspicious beginning. But her natural beauty and subtly beguiling ways had charmed him since the moment she'd moved into his house.

Ty tucked his hands beneath his head and closed his eyes. God's ways were not man's ways. This was just one more bit of proof of that.

He awoke to a tickle under his nose.

Hannah was there, fanning a bit of green fern in his face and humming. He sat up sharply.

"What time is it?"

"Almost five."

"Have you been awake long?"

"About a half hour. I had another piece of my birthday cake. This mountain air makes me famished. I could eat a steak right now and still not be full!"

"We didn't pass all that many restaurants on the way up, but we'll go down another way. I know just the spot."

She must be really hungry, he thought, for she immediately began gathering things up to put in the car. She had dirty feet, tangled hair and a smudge of chocolate frosting on her nose. She was beautiful.

The road down the mountain that he chose was far more winding and precarious than the way they'd come up. He found himself thinking of ways to keep Hannah in his company just a little bit longer, before he had to share her with the rest of his household. Ty found the spot he was looking for and pulled into the parking lot of a low, rambling wooden building with a faded sign that said EATS on it. The building hung just on the edge of a fast-moving creek, which they could hear when Ty opened his window.

"This doesn't look very promising," Hannah said, squinting in the oncoming dusk. Once the sun set it was very dark in the mountains.

"Don't judge a book by its cover." Ty turned off the motor and hopped out. "Come on."

The building didn't look much more promising on the inside, Ty thought, but he remembered it as his grandfather's favorite restaurant. He was willing to give it a chance for old times' sake. A tiny woman wearing an enormous apron and white orthopedic shoes exited the kitchen. She was followed by man in his late fifties wearing jeans and a white T-shirt. The shirt didn't quite make it over his generous belly.

"Tyler Matthews! Is that you?" The woman ripped off her eyeglasses and began to polish them on a corner of the apron. "It's been a month of Sundays since I've seen you."

"Hi, Rita," Ty said.

"You're still a picture of your grandfather only even more handsome! I knew you were going to be that way from the time you were a little boy. You remember my son, Jerome, don't you?"

The man waved a spatula at them.

"I certainly do. Is Eddy here?"

Rita looked sad. "He passed on four years ago. We miss him, but he's having more fun in heaven than the rest of us here on earth. And your grandparents?"

"Gramps is gone, but Lily's still Lily."

"Did you come here for dinner? Or just out of curiosity?"

"Both. I was hoping you might still be here, but I didn't really expect it. I meant to drive up much sooner."

"You're in luck. I've got a rib eye in the back with your name on it. I'll add a portobello for fun and do a little balsamic reduction and we're ready to go. Have a seat anywhere."

Hannah's eyes were big when they sat down. "A balsamic reduction? Here?"

"Again, don't judge a book by its cover.

Rita came up here to open her own place years ago. She was a cook at a classy restaurant and just decided she wanted a more natural life. They don't look fancy, but it's by choice. Lily always said Rita liked to give her money away. A lot of charities have benefited from Rita's success."

"Amazing. Just like this entire day, simply amazing."

She said it again when a pear salad with blue cheese arrived.

"Look at these au gratin potatoes," Ty commented. They were so rich that Rita should have been a cardiologist on call. Next came roasted asparagus with parmesan and sea salt, melt-in-your-mouth steak and a strawberries and crème concoction that left them both begging for mercy.

Hannah leaned back in her chair and groaned with pleasure. "What a perfect spot and meal and company." She bit her lip. When had she decided Ty was perfect for her, anyway?

"More coffee?" Rita wielded a pot.

"That was the perfect meal," Hannah told her. "The most wonderful birthday meal anyone could have. In fact, this has been the ideal birthday." Her face glowed, punctuating her sincerity.

When they left, Ty slipped a hundred-dollar bill beneath the plate as a tip. Rita hugged him good-bye at the door.

"You've got a honey, there," she whispered in his ear. "Don't mess it up."

Rita's warning echoed in Ty's ears all the way down the mountain. There wasn't much to mess up at this point. They were two people exploring their feelings, that's all. Did either of them want it to be more? He needed to find out.

After they'd pulled into the garage and carried the quilt and basket into the house, Hannah, glowing from both sunburn and happiness, turned her face to his. "That was the best day I've had in ages! Thank you so much. I gladly welcome getting a year older for a day like this one."

Gently, Ty lowered his mouth to hers and gave her a sweet kiss. What he'd expected to be pleasant made Fourth of July rockets go off in his head.

Chapter Twenty-Two

"Mr. Matthews, I..."

"What is it, Melanie? I thought I told you I didn't want to be interrupted."

The secretary smiled. "I just wanted you to know that your grandmother has called three more times. She doesn't give up easily, does she?"

"She doesn't give up at all, ever. Did you make sure that she's okay?"

"I did what you said. I asked if I could talk to her caregiver, who said she was fine. She was having a hard time distracting your grandmother from hitting redial. She wanted you to know that the caregiver—Hannah, right?—is going to take Mrs. Matthews to her friend's house for the afternoon, so you can get some work done."

"Thanks, Mel. I promise to improve my mood ASAP Since Lily's going to be busy, why don't you bring in that big stack of files you wanted me to look at?"

He'd done something today that he had never done before in his life. He'd refused to talk to his grandmother. Not refused in a bad way, he told himself. He'd simply told his secretary to screen his calls and tell Lily that he would be tied up today and that he wouldn't be picking up the phone.

Lily, however, wasn't accustomed to being ignored and wasn't about to take no for an answer.

He scraped his hands through his hair, leaned back in his chair and closed his eyes, exhausted. He hadn't slept last night, had done his run an hour early and was out of the house before anyone had stirred. That was fine with him. He didn't want to talk to Hannah until he had his head straightened out. Yesterday he'd walked right into the fact that he was falling in love. There was no denying it anymore. He was head over heels in love with her.

He should have run the other way when she

hit his car. Now she was battering something much more important—his heart.

Ty thought back to yesterday, to their time together in the mountains. It had been a long time since he'd had a day like that. Hannah St. James was easy to love. She was beautiful, sweet, compassionate, smart and somehow both vulnerable and strong. And stuck in the past.

With all that love she had to give, it was natural that Hannah had chosen to be a caregiver—for Danny, Trisha, her clients and now Lily. That provided plenty of people on whom to spread the devotion from that big, warm heart of hers. It satisfied her need to nurture and supported her well-developed fear of giving that love to a man who wasn't Steve.

She'd deny it, he knew, but he could tell when he'd kissed her. Even though she'd responded warmly, she'd held back slightly, like a boxer pulling punches.

The reason he recognized it was because Ty had done it himself. It was not unlike a nervous flyer thinking he could get on an airplane and yet not letting his full weight down. He'd restrained a part of his heart for years, knowing he wouldn't settle for a marriage that was less than the 60-year love affair his grandparents had had. With Hannah, he'd let his guard down and she'd promptly snuck beneath his defenses.

She was only the second woman who'd ever made him think that a marriage like that of Lily and his grandfather was possible. But Hannah was even more skittish than he.

All he could do was hash it out with God and wait for Him to make the next move. If Hannah was ever going to leave her late husband in the past and look to the future, Ty felt it would *have* to be by divine intervention.

When Ty finally did return to the house, Lily wasn't home, but Hannah was.

"She asked Irene to drive her somewhere," Hannah greeted him. She waved her hands helplessly. "I told her I'd do it, but she insisted that Irene be the one and that Danny go with them."

"Now what is she up to?" Ty's voice was weary. He could take anything his job or company threw at him. But this emotional roller coaster these women insisted on bringing him on was going to be his undoing.

"Danny didn't seem to know why she

wanted him to come along either, so I think he's in the dark."

"Worse yet. Whenever Lily scooped me up and my grandfather didn't know what we were up to, it was usually trouble for him."

"What do you mean?"

"Let's just say that no young boy needs a scooter, scuba gear *or* a BB gun."

"You're kidding me."

"My wish was Lily's command much of the time. Both my grandparents loved to spoil me, but at least Gramps had some common sense. Lily never saw the danger in things— only the fun. Danny hasn't been talking about martial arts or downhill skiing, has he?"

"Now you're scaring me, Ty."

He followed her into the kitchen and sat down at the table while she went to the oven and pulled out an apple pie. He was getting accustomed to domestic bliss, he thought. He watched her take out a plate, a fork and an ice-cream scoop and lay them on the counter.

"We'll have pie à la mode as soon as this cools." She sank down into a chair. "I'm feeling the urge for a jolt of pure sugar to keep going. Life's short. Eat dessert first, don't you think?"

"What's happening in Trisha's financial saga?" he asked as he imagined bits of apple in melting vanilla ice cream.

"She called me last night to wish me happy birthday and apologize for not buying me a present. I told her all the present I needed was for her to quit spending money frivolously and get her financial responsibilities figured out. She's trying, I know she is."

"Then what's troubling you?"

"I'd still like to know more about Jason, this boyfriend of hers. She says he's a nice guy and that they aren't serious, just friends."

"And you believe her?"

"I've always believed her until this money fiasco. Now I don't know what to think. She's reminded me that she's still young and that common sense isn't her strong suit."

"Maybe common sense isn't all it's cracked up to be," Ty commented mildly.

Her head snapped up. "What do you mean?"

"Even people with the most common sense need to let go once in a while. Take you, for example."

"Me? What does this have to do with me?"

"You've been logical and sensible for so long that you may not even see how things have changed in your life."

"I don't understand."

"Trisha isn't fourteen anymore. And you aren't married anymore. Your house might not be right for you any longer. You're trying to maintain a life that existed years ago."

"Trisha's just a kid! And my house… Steve and I…" She drooped in her seat. What he was saying was true. Trisha was at the age now when she and Steve had decided to marry. The house was an anchor that held her to the past. Steve was never coming back. Why was she holding on?

Had it been a sad life she'd lived before coming here? A restrained life, perhaps, one without much spontaneity, one in which her filter to every question had been *what would Steve have done?* Or, *what would Steve have thought?* She had rarely asked *what does Hannah want?*

She jumped to her feet, threw open the freezer door, pulled out the vanilla ice-cream bucket and began to saw at the rock-hard contents. Then she gave the ice cream scoop to Ty and cut the pie. She didn't want to think anymore. Maybe if she ate enough ice cream her brain would freeze solid.

It was unnerving, she realized, that Ty watched silently, not commenting on her frenetic behavior. He said nothing as they sat together and devoured half the pie and far too much ice cream.

Hannah was suffering the welcome distraction of a painful brain freeze when they heard footsteps and voices at the front door.

"At least now we'll find out what they've been up to," Ty said.

"Do we even want to know?" She imagined Danny with a pair of nunchakus, a knife or his own race car. Ty's stories had not calmed her mind in any way. What would Steve say if he got hurt…

She stopped herself. It was what she thought that mattered, Hannah reminded herself. She had to live for herself and Danny, to finally learn to embrace the unknown. Those were muscles she hadn't used in a very long time.

"I suppose we'd better see what went on," Ty said grimly. "It could be perfectly harmless—but knowing Lily…"

What they saw when they walked into the entry of the house was harmless, but it had the potential to disrupt this already fragile household and spread chaos wherever it went.

Danny held snuggled in his arms a yellow puppy with a lolling pink tongue and soft brown eyes.

Chapter Twenty-Three

"Danny! What are you doing with that puppy?" Hannah gasped.

"Lily! What have you done now?" Ty glared at the threesome. Danny and Lily looked delighted. Irene was a picture of guilt.

"She made me do it, Mr. Ty. I told her you wouldn't like it, but she wouldn't listen."

"She never does. It's not your fault, Irene. I'll take it from here. Why don't you take Danny to the kitchen with the pup? Hannah made an apple pie."

The woman scooted off toward the kitchen, relief on her face. Danny, blissfully unaware of the undercurrents among the adults, followed her, his arms firmly around the squirming yellow Lab, a dog just like the one Ty had had as a boy.

Danny stopped in front of Ty. "His name is Crackers. Lily said you had a dog named Crackers when you were a boy. She said he loved to eat any kind of cracker. I'll bet this dog likes them, too." He looked hopefully into Ty's eyes. "It's okay if I name my dog Crackers, too, isn't it?"

"Every boy needs a dog, Tyler." Lily fixed those bright blue eyes on him and dared him to challenge her. "Remember how much you loved your dog? You two were inseparable. You wouldn't deny the child such joy, would you?"

This was beyond even his tolerance for Lily's antics. "Did you ask his mother about this? Isn't she the one who should make a decision like that?"

"Oh, she doesn't mind." Lily looked to Hannah for confirmation. "Do you, dear?"

"I… I…" Hannah looked like a deer in the headlights as she blurted what was obviously the first thing that came to her mind, "I'm not sure I can afford a dog, Lily. What if we keep him and I don't find another job after I leave here?"

Lily looked horrified. "You'll be working here, for Ty and me!" She turned toward him. "Won't she, Ty?"

He opened his mouth, but it was Hannah who answered first. "I've only been hired to stay until you're back on your feet, Lily. Soon you won't need me. Look how well you're doing with physical therapy. Irene can cook and clean for you. There won't be a reason for a caregiver. You'll be on your own again."

What was happening to him? Ty wondered. He hadn't felt anything like this in… When *had* he felt like this before? Not since Anita had he been so drawn to a woman. The realization came crashing over him like a tsunami. He'd long believed there was only one soul mate for him and she had died. But now…

"I don't want to be on my own. I want *you*. But we don't need to think about that now. It's going to be fine." Then Lily did as she'd always done—what Ty called "pulling a Scarlett O'Hara." Every time Scarlett ran into something unpleasant, she refused to think about it. Exactly what Lily was doing now.

"I'm that puppy's foster grandmother and Ty is his adoptive uncle. Crackers won't starve. I'll pay for obedience school, if you wish. Besides, we have everything he needs in the car. We bought a kennel, a bed, toys, some grooming tools, a leash, a collar, food, even a toothbrush!" She touched Hannah's hand. "Don't worry, dear. It will be fine. I'm sure of it."

Hannah gave her a weak smile. "Well, thank you for giving my son such a generous gift." A tear slid down one cheek.

Ty couldn't tell if it was inspired by gratitude, anger or fear.

"Oh, honey, don't cry. When I'm fretting about Clara's situation, you tell me to have faith. It'll all work out, Hannah."

Then, demonstrating exactly how far she had come with her therapy, Lily clutched the bars of her walker and took herself to the kitchen, leaving Ty and Hannah alone together.

She grabbed his sleeve. "Oh, Ty, I didn't hurt her feelings, did I? I didn't mean to sound ungrateful. The puppy is a lovely, if overwhelming, gift. It's just that the first thing I thought was that I didn't need another mouth to feed."

"I'll tell her she has to undo this whole thing, Hannah. Don't worry."

"Don't do that! Did you see the look on Danny's face? He's always said he was sure his dad would have bought him a dog someday. He knew I wouldn't because of the hassle, the money. Now he's finally gotten his wish. I can't take that away. I also don't want to hurt Lily. She was only trying to help."

"Her idea of help could sink ships, Hannah. She put you in an impossible situation. Of course, she'll be paying dog support to Danny for the next fifteen years."

She pulled him by the sleeve, indicating he should follow her into the kitchen. "Let's go properly meet the new member of our family. We'll worry about how to pay for him later."

Our family. He liked the sound of that.

The next morning Ty had gone to work, Danny and Lily were closeted in Lily's room with Crackers and Irene was scrubbing the kitchen floor, leaving Hannah at loose ends. It was time to do something she'd been dreading.

Hannah entered the kitchen carrying her purse and keys. "I'm going out for a bit. Call me if there's a problem."

"Only problem I can foresee is that puppy piddling on one of Mr. Ty's wool rugs." Irene shook her head ruefully. "That little critter is about the most adorable thing I've ever seen. I'm just sorry that it wasn't you who drove them to the pet shop instead of me."

"Don't feel bad. None of this was your fault. Besides, Danny is blissfully happy about that pup."

"Just so you know, Miss Lily has been asking me to take her to her friend Clara's house, too. Because she asks during my work day, I always tell her I don't have time."

"Does she do it often?"

"Getting to be more so. She and Clara also talk on the phone but never when you're in the room. I think they're devising something they don't want you to know about."

Lily was a hatchery; if ideas were chicks, she had a million of them.

"I'll talk to Ty about it tonight."

"Mr. Ty is softer with Lily than he really should be. Of course, that's because of that promise he made to his grandfather. Mr. Ty never breaks a promise. His word is good."

Irene paused for a moment, then said thoughtfully, "You make a good team because Lily loves you and listens to reason with you. That makes it easier for Mr. Ty. You've taken a lot of pressure off his shoulders these past weeks. I think we're all dreading the time when you leave, Hannah. You and Danny have brought wonderful life to this house."

Hannah had a myriad of thoughts in her head as she drove downtown to run some errands. Irene had reminded Hannah about the promise he'd made when he was young. She had an ever-growing admiration for the man Ty was.

When she returned to the Matthews' home, Danny was playing with Crackers in the front yard. Lily, ensconced on a lawn chair, watching them with delight. On the sidewalk was a boy about Danny's age. Hannah recognized him—Terrible Kevin of the Black Eye. His gaze was fixed on the squirming, yapping puppy, and his expression was one of longing.

Danny saw the boy about the same time Hannah did. She could see the wheels turning in her little son's head. Then he picked up his puppy and walked slowly toward the other child. A conversation ensued before Danny nodded and the boy reached out his hand to stroke Cracker's head.

Her chest felt clogged with emotion.

Danny was turning out well despite the roller coaster that was her life, not because of it.

Lily waved the boys over so she could meet Danny's new friend.

Hannah began to think of how Danny

would miss Lily terribly when they left. Lily had a doctor's appointment this week. Hannah's best guess was that he'd ask Lily to do a couple more weeks of physical therapy and then pronounce her fit to live in her own home again.

"I saw that Kevin was with you in the yard today," Hannah mentioned casually over dinner.

"Yeah. Me and Ty talked about it one day when you weren't home, didn't we, Ty? He told me about in the Bible where it says we should keep forgiving someone—like seventy times seven. That's four hundred and ninety times! And Ty said God forgives us even more than that so we should act like Him. I told him that was pretty hard, so he said I should just practice turning the other cheek."

Bless Ty's heart!

"I didn't get that turn your other cheek stuff," Danny admitted, helping himself to more mashed potatoes. "I figure that if you turn your other cheek on a bully, he'll just slug you there, too, but I tried it."

"How did it work out?" Ty asked.

"Pretty good. Kevin's mom won't let him

have a pet. I could tell it made him sad, so I asked him if he wanted to pet Crackers. He got nicer after that. He really likes dogs so he was pretty happy that I'd let him play with mine. He's gonna come over tomorrow and we're going to teach Crackers to fetch. Kevin apologized, too—for that stuff he said about you, Mom. He's okay, I guess."

The boy said it matter-of-factly. His nemesis was becoming his friend. Hannah and Ty exchanged glances. She smiled and gave him a thumbs-up. He winked back in a secret exchange between them.

Hannah felt tears burning in her throat. Ty Matthews was the only father figure Danny had had in a very long time.

Hannah went upstairs to tell Danny to get ready for bed, but to her surprise he was already in his room, teeth brushed, pajamas on and a book in front of him. Flat on his belly, feet splayed, Crackers was sleeping soundly on his dog bed.

"What got into you? Going to bed without being told a half-dozen times? Are you sick?" Hannah pretended to feel his forehead for fever.

Danny grinned at her. "Lily told me if I'd rest up tonight, she'd have Irene take us to the pet store again. They're having a sale on dog accessories."

"Danny, do you know what dog accessories are?"

"Not really, but I bet with Lily it's going to be fun!"

Suddenly, an image of Ty at Danny's age, trusting his grandmother to plan their next outing, sprang into her mind. It was no wonder that Ty loved her so much or pampered her so lavishly. If only her own parents had been able to meet Danny.

She fought back the tears, kissed her son on the forehead and left the room.

Lord, You are the Maker of miracles. I know You have a plan for me. Please give me an inkling of what it might be. Show me what I'm supposed to do first.

"Are those tears?"

At the bottom of the staircase she swung toward Ty's office. He was framed in the doorway, sleeves rolled up, collar undone, ready to get back to work. He gestured her inside.

She followed him inside even though she didn't feel like talking right now.

Without comment, he pointed her toward the long leather couch. Then he picked up a remote and switched on the gas fireplace, which sparked to life. Turning to her again, he took the plaid throw draped over the back of the sofa and laid it over her as she sat, feet beneath her, curled into the leather arm.

"Thank you." Between her nerves and the coolness of the evening, she was shivering.

"Maybe it will help if you talk about it."

"You're sweet to ask, but I don't think so."

He nodded and didn't speak. Ironically, it was his lack of pressure that persuaded her to open up.

"I'm just feeling sorry for myself. Danny's so fond of Lily. I was thinking how bad he'll feel when Lily's well and we leave here. By the way, Danny and Lily have a plan for tomorrow."

"Lily is the Pied Piper of children," Ty said. "She should have taught school. She could have persuaded her students to study anything and convinced them they were still having fun.

"Also, I notice that thanks to your good care, she's really improved her walking the past couple weeks."

"She doesn't need me anymore—or at least she won't soon."

"You think she's doing that well?" He looked delighted. "That's great news!"

His pleasure at the return of Lily's good health depressed her mightily. It reminded her of her imminent departure.

Tears began to roll down her cheeks. She was so tired of trying to hold everything together—Trisha's irresponsible behavior, parenting Danny, her finances and her job. She couldn't make the tears stop.

It had grown dark outside as night fell, closeting them together in a world of their own. Suddenly, Hannah found herself enveloped in strong yet gentle arms. She sank into Ty's warm broad chest and sobbed even more.

Unspeaking, he held her tight.

Finally spent, she sagged against him and closed her eyes.

Then she felt Ty's fingers beneath her chin. He tipped her head and Hannah felt his lips on hers, a kiss that was both comforting and passionate. She responded with emotions she didn't know she still had. Emotions she believed she'd lost many years before. Instead, they had been waiting for the man who could ignite them again. But why had this happened now, when her own needs already had to be put on the back burner for the sake of Danny and Trisha? She had so much baggage and so little else to bring to a relationship. It wasn't fair to Ty. It wasn't fair to anyone.

Then he kissed her again and nothing else mattered.

Chapter Twenty-Four

As they sat there, wrapped in each other's arms, they heard a cry. Lily.

They both ran up to the second floor. Danny met them at the top of the stairs. His blond hair was tousled and his cheeks rosy with sleep. Hannah put her arm around the child.

Ty pushed into Lily's room. She was sitting upright in bed. The pink scarf she wore to protect her hairdo was askew and those bright blue eyes were huge in her face.

"What's wrong, Gram?"

"It's Clara. She fell out of bed." Lily sounded frantic. "She knocked the phone off the side table as she fell so she was able to reach it. She's been calling out but can't rouse either her sister, Margaret, or her nephew. Clara thinks she may have broken her hip!"

"We'll call 911," Hannah said as she dug her cell phone out of her pocket.

Tears sprang to Lily's eyes. "Please, we have to help her!"

When Hannah went into Lily's room the next morning, the older woman was just hanging up her phone.

"Did you hear anything about Clara?"

"I just talked to her. She's groggy, having had surgery to repair her hip only last night. They told her she'd have to move into a nursing home for a while and have physical therapy when she leaves the hospital. She doesn't want to go back to her sister's house, of course, but she's not sure what to do next. I'll have to discuss it with Ty. We need to find a safe, permanent place for her and I've got something in mind."

Later that day, Hannah approached Ty.

"I heard from Lily that you said that Clara could come to your house when she got out of the hospital," Hannah said softly. "That was terribly generous of you, but have you really thought it through?"

"I have, actually. Lily loves Clara and vice versa. What's more, I know Lily will want to go back to her own home as soon as she can. Lily is almost ready to go home. It's a big place. I plan to suggest that Clara move there with Lily—if you'll agree to be there with them. It would provide Clara with someplace more pleasant than she's been and she and Lily could keep each other company."

"And out of *your* hair?" Hannah teased. "I think it's a wonderful idea."

"I thought about that," he admitted sheepishly. "Lily needs companionship. It might be the answer to a number of problems."

"What do you think Lily will say?"

"It's more about what Clara's sister and nephew say. I'm sure they were collecting money for having her at their house."

"Clara is clearheaded and capable of making her own decisions."

"Let's hope so."

Hannah drove Lily to visit Clara nearly every day. That had become much easier now that Lily was accustomed to her cane and more mobile. Sometimes they also picked up Clara's sister, Margaret. The old ladies delighted in each other and never ran out of things to discuss. Since "rescuing" Clara, Lily had been radiant with happiness. And because she had free access to her friend every single day, Clara was blooming under the attention. Her strength was returning by leaps and bounds.

On the days Ty worked at home, he always ensured that Lily and Hannah visited Clara to make sure he had some uninterrupted hours in which to take care of his business. Hannah was willing to oblige.

"Guess what Danny taught me," Lily said as they drove toward the care center. She was wearing a beige straw hat festooned with flowers and fruit.

"That could be any number of things. He's taught Crackers to sit, stay and heel, after all."

Lily waved her hand cheerfully. "Oh, he could never teach me to obey commands of any kind—Ty can tell you about that."

She turned toward Hannah, her blue eyes twinkling dangerously. "He taught me to shop online."

That struck fear into even Hannah's heart. Lily, the web and a credit card were a dangerous combination.

"I didn't know Danny had been shopping on the internet," Hannah mumbled, mentally making it a priority to check her computer settings so he couldn't find things even more dangerous on the web.

"But I figured out how to 'search' all by myself."

Hannah hid a smile. "What have you looked up?" Hats, probably, or purses, two of Lily's favorite purchases.

"Foster care, state-licensed private homes. The things I've asked you about the past few weeks. I'm learning all about them.

"Adult foster care involves private homes that take in a few, maybe five or six, elderly people and provide them help so they can live as independently as possible in a comfortable, homelike setting. People can bring their own furniture, pictures and anything else they wanted with which to decorate their rooms. It offers an opportunity to be involved with a family, have around-the-clock companionship and a chance to get out into the garden or bake cookies if they want. Isn't that wonderful?"

Lily had done her homework. "I think it's a great option, Lily, but places like that are hard to find."

"It sounds like a perfect answer for someone like Clara. It's more affordable than a nursing home but is still licensed and well-regulated. It would be clean and pleasant."

"And just what do you propose to do with this information?" Hannah asked.

"I've already done it. When Ty came up to have coffee with me this morning, I shared what I'd learned. I also told him that I wanted to turn my house into a foster-care facility. It's much too big for me anyway. I have no desire to live there alone any longer. I'm getting to be an old lady, hard as it is for me to believe. Then both Clara and her sister could come to live with me. And there would still be room for two more ladies."

"It's a wonderful thought, but a foster facility means you move in with a family unit with a caregiver that is qualified to run such a place."

"I already have that."

"Who? Ty? I hardly think…"

"You! I know you have financial issues and no job lined up after this one. You can sell your house and move in with me and be our caregiver. This way you won't have to look for another job. You can hire whatever staff you need. Danny will not only have his own room, but also all my gardens to run in and an entire playroom. He'll love it." Lily smiled wistfully. "And I'll have another little boy in my life."

"But I can't."

"Why not?"

"It's a huge change, Lily. Danny and I…" She'd spent her lifetime trying to keep things the same—and now this.

"You'll earn a considerable amount, Hannah. I don't need any more money. I know you'll have to hire staff, a housekeeper and cook, but after expenses you can have everything else. No money need to come to me at all. Having Clara, and perhaps even Margaret, under my roof and you and Danny in my life is more payment to me than you'll ever know."

Hannah felt herself gasping for air. "You'd need a lot of space to manage something like this."

Lily peered at her. "Hannah, have you ever *seen* my house?"

"No, I…"

"Let's drive by it before we visit Clara at the hospital. Then you'll understand that everything will be fine." She gave Hannah an address and took out the cell phone she'd insisted on getting after Clara's fall. "I'll let them know we're coming."

Numbly, Hannah drove to the house, trying to grasp all that Lily was proposing.

"Turn here," Lily ordered, pointing to a set of large arched gates. She waved at the gentleman in the guard house who gave the old woman a broad smile.

"Nice to see you again, Miss Lily. Are you moving back home soon?"

"I hope so, Ted," Lily called cheerily out the window. She turned back to Hannah, who was staring at the mountainous houses on the block, many bigger than some apartment houses. "Turn right. My home is at the end of the cul-de-sac."

Three large homes loomed before them. The center one, which Lily had indicated, looked like a brick English manor house with gardens spread out on all sides. The drive up to the house was a horseshoe-shaped road built of brick pavers. When they reached the massive double wooden doors, they glided open to reveal a small woman with merry eyes and a tall, slender gentleman, both close to seventy.

"Miss Lily! You're back!"

"The Jacobs have been with me for years," Lily explained. "They've kept the house running while I've been at Ty's. Come in and I'll give you a tour."

By the time Hannah had been through the drawing room, the parlor, the massive dining and living rooms and the kitchen with its professional stove and refrigerators, the eight bedrooms, each with its own bath, she was walking in an amazed stupor.

This place wasn't a house—it was a hotel!

"We should be able to make it work, don't you think?" Lily inquired after they'd returned to the car. "You and Danny should be able to find a place to be comfortable. The third-floor suite, maybe. That's large and private. There's a playroom up there that used to be Ty's. Or I can build something."

"Lily, I had no idea. I thought Ty's house was a mansion. But this..."

"Let's just say that my husband was a very successful man. Railroads, bridge construction and some exceptionally wise investments along with the import/export business Ty runs. He had the resources to pamper me and Ty. Fortunately Ty turned out to be levelheaded and modest. He's always told me that I should use my big house for a higher purpose and now I've found one."

Hannah, who was rarely at a loss for words, couldn't think of a thing to say.

Chapter Twenty-Five

Ty paced the floor, waiting for Lily and Hannah's return. He was nervous as a cat in a dog pound conjecturing how Hannah was responding to Lily's proposal.

Hannah had told him only yesterday that she'd decided to sell her house. He recalled her words. "I realize now that it's time to sell the house—and for all of us to move on. I can't live on memories any longer. I've hung on too long already. The house and Steve are part of my past. Steve wouldn't have wanted me to stop my life like I have. I did it because it was familiar and it felt safer than making the changes I should have. I've prayed about it a lot lately and I'm sure this is the right thing to do."

When he'd offered to help her, she'd been

firm. "I don't want you picking up the messy pieces of my life and enabling me like I enabled Trisha. I need to do this on my own." She'd touched his sleeve. "But I'll always love you for offering."

I'll always love you.

He'd hung on to that. He was in love with her, there was no doubt about that. It had taken him a long time to realize that the woman Hannah reminded him of most was his own grandmother. Lily was compassionate, generous, honest, transparent, loyal and loving—all the attributes embodied in this tiny redhead. And he was very much like his grandfather. If he was looking for a woman to create a marriage with, like that of his grandparents, Hannah was the key. He desperately wanted to take care of her, to give her all the things she'd never had, to make her smile. Only now, after all these years, did he fully and completely understand his grandfather's passion for Lily.

Even better, she loved Lily almost as much as he did. What was a more perfect fulfillment of his grandfather's dying wish than a team like he and Hannah to make Lily's last years happy?

But Hannah, despite a few pleasant lapses,

held herself professionally aloof from him. For once in his life, Ty Matthews was worried—if he offered her his love, would she return it?

"Man up," he muttered. "Risk it."

There was something he'd considered, a signal of sorts, but it had felt too silly—until now. With a determined set to his jaw, Ty went to the garage, picked up the piece Hannah had asked him to store for her weeks ago and began to gently unwrap it.

Hannah wondered where the pavement had gone as she exited her car at Ty's place. Was she just floating above it on a cloud of excitement and happiness? She could see already that Lily's plan was not only feasible but supremely doable. The house even had an elevator. No physical changes would be needed to turn the place into an elderly-friendly space. Lily had already picked Clara's room—right next to her own. Margaret, if she decided to come, would have the room on the other side of her sister. Her son, John, would have no reason to protest their move. He could mess up his own house and eat fried chicken and pizza to his heart's delight. That left only two rooms to fill, an easy task, Hannah knew, in a place like Lily's.

She and Danny would have an apartment of their own at Lily's. She already knew that her son would be ecstatic to remain close to his adopted grandmother. He was calling Lily "Grams" just as Ty did.

What's more, it was far past time to push Trisha out of the nest. Without the burden of the house, Hannah could still pay for her sister's education, but Trisha would have to be responsible for the rest. She'd stumble, no doubt, and Hannah would have the where-withal to bail her out if it were necessary, but she wasn't going to tell Trisha that. It was time to cut the apron strings that Hannah had tied so tightly after their parents had died. She wanted Trisha to blossom into independence and begin to live her own life. Her only regret was that she hadn't allowed it sooner.

She helped Lily out of the car but was oblivious to her surroundings until Lily pointed an arthritic finger toward one of the flower beds. "What's that?"

Hannah's gaze followed Lily's pointing finger.

Her garden gnome, the one she'd taken from her house and stored in Ty's garage, was tucked neatly next to a shrub, moss roses scattered at his feet. He looked as if he had belonged there all the time, happy in his new setting.

She didn't know whether to laugh or to cry. Even the gnome was more flexible than she'd been. He looked perfectly satisfied with his change in location. In fact, he looked right at home.

Irene met them at the door and whisked Lily off to the kitchen for a reviving pot of tea. That left Hannah to greet Ty when he appeared at his office door.

"What do you think?" he asked. He sounded excited and oddly nervous.

"It's fantastic. The perfect place for what Lily has planned."

"Will you do it? Work for her, I mean?"

"I'd be a fool to turn her down. It would be a bridge, a place for us to live after I sell my house, and the perfect job for me. It's more than I ever dreamed." She heard her voice break. "It's a God thing, Ty. He's given me the desire of my heart."

"Good. I was hoping you'd accept." Ty sighed in relief. "I didn't want you to leave our lives."

She looked. "You didn't?"

"Not at all."

"I didn't want to leave either, not really." She refrained from adding *not ever.* "By the way, why is my garden gnome sitting in your flower bed?"

"About that…" Ty took a deep breath. "I'd like him to stay there, if you don't mind."

"But he's my gnome."

"Maybe I could adopt him."

She stared at him, confused.

"You know, when I marry his mother. Then he could stay in my flower bed forever." He stepped forward and circled his arms around her. "Hannah, will you marry me?"

She felt the sweet warmth of his breath on her cheek and succumbed to the urge to lean against his chest. This, she knew as he kissed her hair, was truly the biggest and best thing for which her heart had ever longed. She'd simply never dreamed that deep, true love could strike her twice in a lifetime.

A slow, wide smile spread across her face as she buried it in his chest. "I could manage that. Anything for the children—Danny and the gnome, I mean."

"Do you think Danny would agree to be my best man?" Ty whispered through a cloud of red hair, his lips near her ear.

She tipped her face to his. "Only if Lily will be my bridesmaid. I'm sure she and Trisha can find lovely matching dresses."

"I can answer for her, Hannah. It's a definite 'yes.' Lily's been asking me when I was going to get around to proposing. She'll be relieved to know I finally got up the nerve."

"Nerve? Since when have you lacked nerve?" Hannah teased.

"Just since your answer was the most important thing in my life, that's all." He put a gentle finger beneath her chin and tipped it up. "You aren't the only one God has blessed, Hannah. He's given me things I didn't even know were missing in my life."

Then he lowered his lips to hers.

Just as he did so, Lily burst into the room, her cane tapping on the floor. "Well, it's about time! Can I assume we have a wedding to plan?"

Ty broke the kiss and sighed. Hannah felt his warm sweet breath on her cheek. "Yes, Gram. Now leave us alone."

Lily cackled with glee. "Of course! You lovebirds take the day off. Have fun. I'm going to get on the internet. I've been dying to research flowers for the wedding."

Even though Ty groaned softly near her ear, everything was going to work out now, Hannah realized. Every little thing.

Epilogue

Ty's gaze scanned the church as he waited at the front for the moment to arrive. His collar itched and the cummerbund was unfamiliar at his waist. He caught Lily's eye as she stood across from him. She'd been over the moon when Hannah had asked her to join Trisha, the maid of honor, at the altar as Hannah's matron of honor.

Packages from prominent department and specialty stores had begun arriving at the house almost immediately—bridesmaid dresses in every color and style. Lily and Trisha had spent hours in front of the mirror modeling garments until not only his, but Hannah's eyes glazed over. It would have appeared that Lily was going to be the center of attention had she not accompanied Hannah to Denver's most exclusive bridal shops to choose her wedding dress.

At first Hannah had protested, insisting she wanted nothing more than a simple, inexpensive sheath, but Lily—as usual—had prevailed. The dress had become the subject of many secret conversations to which Ty was not privy.

"You can't see the dress until she walks down the aisle," his future sister-in-law had told him. "And she'll blow your mind. Just wait and see."

Hannah already blew his mind—in fact, his entire life.

Then Ty fixed his eyes on the back of the church, unaware of anything but the empty arched doorway through which his bride would come.

Suddenly she was there, a vision in cream-colored lace that skirted her curves and sparkled with elaborate beading. Danny was at her side in his pint-size tuxedo, looking very self-important in the role to which he'd been assigned—giving his mother away at the altar. Tyler Matthews, cool, calm international businessman, forgot to breathe.

* * *

Bless his heart, Hannah thought as she looked at her broad-shouldered, dark-haired, incredibly handsome groom-to-be. He'd taken to fatherhood like a duck to water. In the days since their engagement, Ty and Danny had lived in a constant flurry of playing catch, improving golf swings, playing board games and watching old television reruns that they both loved.

Loving her son was the quickest way to her heart, and that was only one of the ways Ty had embedded himself there. Sometimes she thought her heart might burst with joy. God had worked a miracle in bringing them to this day.

She felt Danny tug on her hand and heard the music swell. Hannah took a small step forward.

It was time to become Mrs. Tyler Matthews.

* * * * *

If you enjoyed Judy Baer's book, be sure to check out the other books this month from Love Inspired.

Dear Reader,

I grew up as an only child of older parents. It was perfectly natural for me to hang out with people a generation or two—even three—older than myself. My parents' friends were my friends and I thought they were wonderful.

Spending time in the company of my elders taught me that even though the body may age, the mind and spirit remain young. Someone is not less appealing or exciting because they are "old." Wrinkles and gray hair may hide a young, playful mind. Tyler Matthews, hero of *The Bachelor Boss,* understands this very well. He is responsible for the care of his independent, feisty and stubborn grandmother Lily when she breaks her foot. Lily hates being bored and expects Tyler to keep her entertained. That's when Tyler hires Hannah St. James to relieve some of the pressure on him. He invites her and her eight-year-old son to live in his home while she is caring for Lily. Widowed when her son was young, Hannah hasn't let herself fall in love again, but living under the same roof as Ty awakens something in her that she hasn't felt for a long time. Ty has suffered his own loss, and neither of them cares to have their heart broken again. Lily, however, ready for great-grandchildren, has other ideas.

I thoroughly enjoyed writing the character of Lily and her interaction with the "younger" generation. The elderly can teach the young and certainly the young can teach the aged. God has given us the gift of family so that we may hear the stories and learn the lessons of generations. I hope you enjoyed Ty and Hannah's journey to love.

I'd love to hear from you. Feel free to write to me at Love Inspired, 233 Broadway, Suite 1001, New York, New York, 10279.

Judy

Questions for Discussion

1. What are your experiences with your own grandparents? Did you have the privilege of knowing them or were they already gone when you were born? What was your relationship to them? What are your memories?

2. What is the most unforgettable trait about each of them?

3. Have you known anyone like Lily—bossy, endearing, meddling and lovable all at once? How do you handle someone who drives you crazy one moment and melts your heart the next?

4. Tyler is an adoring grandson. Do you think he goes too far to keep his grandmother happy—or not far enough? What do you think he should be doing instead?

5. Hannah raised her younger sister after their parents died. Do you think she did a good job? Imagine how it might be if at twenty-four you became the parent to

a much younger sibling. What would you do differently?

6. Hannah's son, Danny, and Lily become the best of friends. What do you know about relationships between the very young and the very old? Do you imagine yourself someday befriending young people in that way?

7. Lily buys Danny a puppy without asking the permission of his mother. Hannah, who knows that she might lose her house, was unhappy but unable to break her little boy's heart by sending it back. How would you handle such a situation?

8. Trisha has no idea how to handle money. She has little concept about what income vs. expenses mean for her until she gets herself and her sister into financial trouble. As a young adult, how were you with money? What do you know now that you wished you'd learned then?

9. God is woven into the fabric of these characters' everyday lives. How does He fit into your life right now?

LARGER-PRINT BOOKS!

GET 2 FREE LARGER-PRINT NOVELS PLUS 2 FREE MYSTERY GIFTS

Love Inspired

Larger-print novels are now available...

LILP11B

Love Inspired®
SUSPENSE
RIVETING INSPIRATIONAL ROMANCE

Watch for our series of edge-
of-your-seat suspense novels.
These contemporary tales
of intrigue and romance
feature Christian characters
facing challenges to their faith...
and their lives!

AVAILABLE IN REGULAR
& LARGER-PRINT FORMATS

For exciting stories that reflect traditional values,
visit:
www.ReaderService.com